The moment his mouth touched hers, Claire felt the sparks she always had.

Nick's arm tightened around her waist and his mouth pressed more firmly, opening hers as he really kissed her, a deep, sexy kiss that stopped her worrying and shut off memories of their past and the big problem she faced.

With her heart pounding, she clung to Nick and kissed him in return, knowing it was folly, but unable to stop. She was swept back in time, into memories of Nick's steamy, passionate kisses that had stolen her heart so quickly—something she couldn't let happen again.

When they moved apart, he was breathing as hard as she. His kiss had shaken her, igniting desire that burned through worry, but as she faced him again, his blue eyes filled with curiosity. Nick was an intelligent man and he had already picked up on something.

How would she tell him about his son?

* * *

The Rancher's Secret Son is part of the Lone Star Legends series by *USA TODAY* bestselling author Sara Orwig!

Dear Reader,

This story involves love, strong family ties, a secret that has to be revealed and a Christmas transformed for two families. This is about another Milan influenced by an old family legend—a legend that in early generations became a family tradition.

While billionaire Nick Milan prefers life as a rancher, he yields to his father's influence to uphold family tradition. Nick is an attorney following a rising political career, only to find his life changed by Claire Prentiss, the woman he once loved. Thrown together by circumstances, they are caught in an intense attraction. Since the reasons they couldn't marry earlier have grown stronger, both Nick and Claire are certain they should fight falling in love again to avoid a greater hurt than before.

Welcome to another story about the Milans and Calhouns of West Texas and the men and women they love.

Best wishes to you,

Sara Orwig

THE RANCHER'S
SECRET SON

—

SARA ORWIG

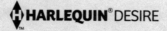

If you purchased this book without a cover you should be aware that this book is stolen property. It was reported as "unsold and destroyed" to the publisher, and neither the author nor the publisher has received any payment for this "stripped book."

Recycling programs
for this product may
not exist in your area.

ISBN-13: 978-0-373-73430-6

The Rancher's Secret Son

Copyright © 2015 by Sara Orwig

All rights reserved. Except for use in any review, the reproduction or utilization of this work in whole or in part in any form by any electronic, mechanical or other means, now known or hereinafter invented, including xerography, photocopying and recording, or in any information storage or retrieval system, is forbidden without the written permission of the publisher, Harlequin Enterprises Limited, 225 Duncan Mill Road, Don Mills, Ontario M3B 3K9, Canada.

This is a work of fiction. Names, characters, places and incidents are either the product of the author's imagination or are used fictitiously, and any resemblance to actual persons, living or dead, business establishments, events or locales is entirely coincidental.

This edition published by arrangement with Harlequin Books S.A.

For questions and comments about the quality of this book, please contact us at CustomerService@Harlequin.com.

® and TM are trademarks of Harlequin Enterprises Limited or its corporate affiliates. Trademarks indicated with ® are registered in the United States Patent and Trademark Office, the Canadian Intellectual Property Office and in other countries.

HARLEQUIN®

™ www.Harlequin.com

Printed in U.S.A.

Sara Orwig lives in Oklahoma. She has a patient husband who will take her on research trips anywhere, from big cities to old forts. She is an avid collector of Western history books. With a master's degree in English, Sara has written historical romance, mainstream fiction and contemporary romance. Books are beloved treasures that take Sara to magical worlds, and she loves both reading and writing them.

Visit her Author Profile page at Harlequin.com, or saraorwig.com, for more titles.

With many thanks to Stacy Boyd,
who made this book possible.

Also thank you to Maureen Walters,
and with love to my family.

One

Nick Milan looked at the small white business card attached to the contract on his desk, and a shock ran through him. Just like last night, when he'd first seen it, he was shaken clear to his core.

"Claire Prentiss."

Just saying the name brought a shadowy image to his mind. An image of a willowy, black-haired, brown-eyed beauty writhing in his arms. The mental picture tortured him, and he pushed the card to the back of his desk. It was almost time to meet his client for what should have been a routine real estate closing. With Claire as the broker, however, it would be far from routine.

The depth of his reaction to the prospect of seeing her again shocked him. It had been four years since he'd held her, four years since he'd been in love with her. Four years since she had rejected his marriage proposal and they'd gone their separate ways. For a long time after the bitter fight that had led to their breakup he'd been hurt and angry with Claire. But that was over. So, why was he still affected by the mere sight of her name?

Claire Prentiss was part of his past now, he tried telling himself. Out of his life for years. She was probably married with kids, helping her grandfather run his real estate agency and still using her maiden name because of business.

Judging by the way his hand shook as he turned his wrist to check his watch, he needed more convincing.

Nick picked up the contract and placed it in his briefcase, snapping it shut the way he wished he could shut out the painful memories of Claire. He had to now. He had work to do.

As he drove to his appointment, he forced himself to focus on the closing, which he wished now he had never agreed to do. But it was for a friend. Paul Smith had called late yesterday afternoon, suddenly deciding he needed his attorney present. Nick had agreed, not knowing Claire would be involved. Why would he? She was a Houston broker. What was she doing closing a deal in Dallas? His friend had sent the contract to Nick's office immediately after the call, but Nick had been too busy to read it until evening which is why he'd taken it home with him. If it hadn't been close to midnight and way too late for his friend to get another attorney, he would have backed out there and then.

He'd spent a sleepless night dreading this meeting and being tormented by memories that would best be forgotten.

In minutes he parked the car and stepped out into a chilly, brisk December wind that whipped through the tall buildings in downtown Dallas. Entering the lobby of one of the office towers, he met up with Paul and shook hands, swallowing the words he longed to say: *Get another lawyer to represent you.* Instead, together they rode the elevator to a commercial real estate office on the twenty-seventh floor.

As they entered through the double glass doors, Bruce Jernigan, the agent who represented the buyer, came forward to meet them.

"If you gentlemen will come this way, we'll get started. As you know, the seller was hospitalized and could not appear, so she has legal representation in her real estate broker." He led them down a long corridor to the conference room, where he opened a door onto a room with dark wood paneling.

Nick's gaze went to Claire instantly. Standing beside the table, she gripped it as her eyes widened and all color left her face. He realized she hadn't known he would attend the meeting until this moment. While he wasn't as shocked as Claire appeared to be, his insides clutched. He felt as if the breath had been punched from his lungs. As he approached and extended his hand, he couldn't drag his eyes from her. At twenty-four she had been beautiful. Now she was breathtaking.

Regaining her poise, she pulled down the jacket of her tailored navy business suit, then shook his hand. "So, we meet again." Her voice hid the tremble he felt in her fingers before she pulled away. "It's nice to see you again, Nick. Mr. Jernigan had just started to tell me that the buyer was bringing an attorney. I had no idea it would be you."

The moment their hands touched, he'd felt an electric current, another reaction that surprised him. Since losing Karen and their unborn baby two years ago, he had been numb around women, his heart shut away, even his physical urges flatlined. Until now. Seeing Claire elicited emotional and physical responses that shook him. He wanted neither of those reactions.

As he moved to a chair beside his client, his gaze roamed over Claire. Tall, with dark brown eyes and raven locks that fell to her shoulders, Claire looked more sophisticated than when he had known her years ago. He didn't have to look at the label to know she wore a designer suit. When her jacket swung open as she sat, her waist looked as tiny as he remembered.

"Let's get down to business." Mr. Jernigan's voice cut into his thoughts.

For the next half hour it was an effort to concentrate on business and not study Claire or let his thoughts drift to the past. He was grateful for a short break while they waited for copies to be made of various documents. He stepped out of the room to check with his office and take calls, then returned, walking to the table where Claire again stood.

When she reached for a glass, he picked up the water pitcher. She glanced up at him and he felt another electrifying tingle as her gaze met his. Smiling at her, he steadied her hand and poured her water, aware of his fingers over her warm, slender hand.

"Thank you," she said.

"So, you're still working at your grandfather's agency," Nick said, recalling how dedicated she had been to her family and assuming she still was. "Is he as active?"

She shook her head. "No, Grandpa's had a heart attack and another little stroke. He had been grooming me to take over the agency for a long time, and I did so a couple of years ago."

"It was a good thing you're loyal and stuck with your family. How's the business going?"

"Fine," she said, smiling slightly. "I'm happy that the business has grown and we have a lot of good listings. I suppose your parents, especially your dad, are pleased with your legal and political career."

"Yes, they are. Especially my dad. So you know I'm in the Texas legislature?"

"Yes. You do make the papers now and then," she said, her cheeks getting slightly more rosy. Was she embarrassed for him to discover she had kept up with his career? He was pleased she had, even though he had always tried to push thoughts of her aside and to avoid knowing much about her.

"You look great," he said, smiling at her, and she smiled in return, a cool smile, yet it sent another wave of longing crashing over him.

"Thank you. I'm sure you enjoy being a Texas State Representative. I know the Texas legislature isn't in session until January, so do you live here in Dallas when you're not in Austin?"

"Yes." He glanced over her head to see everyone returning to the table and he knew soon they would be through and she would be gone.

He didn't know what prompted the feeling, but he didn't want to part. As he glanced back at her, her thickly lashed eyes were gazing at him, making his pulse quicken. Impulsively, he said, "Come to dinner with me tonight and we can catch up."

Her eyes widened. "Do you think that will be of concern to your wife?"

He felt as if he had suffered a blow to his solar plexus. Drawing in a tight breath, he said, "I didn't realize that you didn't know... I'm widowed. My wife was killed in a car wreck two years ago. She was pregnant."

All color drained from Claire's face as her eyes opened wider, looking enormous and panic-stricken, a reaction that shocked him. A visible tremor ran through her and she put a hand on the table to steady herself. He reached out to grab her arm. Odd, he thought. Why would she have such a profound reaction to the news that he was a widower?

"Are you all right?"

Instantly her face flushed and she appeared to pull herself together. She withdrew her arm from his grasp and stood up straight. "Yes. Sorry, it's just…personal. I—" She seemed to think better of what she was about to say and changed her course, giving him a pat response. "I'm sorry for your loss."

He became aware that everyone was getting seated around the table and their time together was over. "Come to dinner with me. It'll be an early evening."

She stared at him so long he wondered whether she heard him, but then she nodded. "Yes. I'll give you my cell phone number after the meeting. We better sit now, because the others are waiting."

While she moved away from him, he saw the color slowly return to her face. He sat down, stacking papers in front of him, but nothing could keep him from wondering about her strong reaction.

What had happened in her life? Had she been in love with someone who was also killed? He couldn't guess why he had gotten such a startling response from her to the news that he had lost Karen and his unborn baby. Tonight he would probably hear why, over dinner.

An hour later, the closing was finalized. As everyone milled around and talked, Nick circled the table to Claire.

She held out a piece of paper. "Here's my cell phone number and the hotel where I'm staying."

"How's seven?"

"That's fine, Nick," she said. "I—"

His cell phone buzzed and he held up his index finger to get her to wait a second. He needed to take the call. In two minutes, when he turned back around, Claire was gone.

Nick finished up with his client, then he returned to the office and was inundated with calls. It was after five before he had a chance to think about the evening and Claire. Now he wondered why he had asked her to dinner in the first place. Their parting four years ago had been so painful, so final. Why was he putting himself in a position to relive those agonizing moments? It still hurt to think back to that time in his life. He'd been so driven to succeed in his career and in politics—was even more so now—and he'd needed a wife who, above all else, supported him in those goals, even if it meant leaving behind her own family obligations. Claire had been deeply involved in her family and their lives had been her priority—and apparently they still were, seeing as how she had taken over the agency from her grandfather.

Nothing had changed.

Tonight he'd make their dinner short. A brief catch-up and then goodbye. It was all he could handle.

Claire ordered flowers for her client and had a congratulatory note attached. It wasn't until she was back in her hotel room and had texted her client that she had a moment to think about the events of the day and her upcoming dinner date.

Instantly, she thought about Nick's news that he was a widower. She could hear his voice. "*I didn't realize that you didn't know... I'm widowed. My wife was killed in a car wreck two years ago. She was pregnant.*"

Nick's wife and unborn baby had been killed. When he announced that, Claire's head had spun and for a moment she'd thought she was going to faint. She wished with her whole heart she had never come to Dallas. Claire ran her hand across her eyes and sighed. She had never dreamed she would encounter Nick.

Why had she agreed to go to dinner with him? Tears stung her eyes. She didn't want to get involved with him again—yet she had no choice. She still hurt over the breakup with him four years ago. Nick hadn't understood her family obligations then. He had simply wanted her to leave them behind to devote her life to him. She'd had to walk away and she didn't want to draw him back into her life now, when she faced life-changing problems far worse than she'd faced before.

She picked up her purse and took out her wallet.

Her heart twisted as she looked at the picture of her son. Nick's son. The child Nick knew nothing about. She looked into the same blue eyes beneath the same dark brown hair as Nick's. She had once loved his father with her whole heart, until their breakup had torn her to pieces. After their breakup she had learned she was carrying Nick's baby.

She hadn't told him right away because she'd needed time to make decisions. Their last time together had been painful, filled with terrible accusations that couldn't be taken back. The memories echoed in her mind even now. He had proposed and she had asked him how they would ever work out being married when she had to take care of her ailing mother and help her grandfather with his business in Houston. Nick had expected her to move to Washington, DC, to be the society wife he had dreamed about—something she could never be.

Nick had accused her of being so wrapped up in her family she couldn't love anyone else. But it wasn't like that at all. Her mother had been diagnosed with Parkinson's and her grandfather had suffered a mild stroke. They needed her the same way Nick needed his father's approval.

She could almost hear herself say those words to him. She accused him of going into law only because of a family tradition. All Milan males had become lawyers. Yet he couldn't see that he was more tied to his family than she was to hers.

Her last night with Nick had been bitter and hurtful, each of them flinging accusations until he had stormed out, slamming the door, and she had let him go, knowing it was over forever between them. Brokenhearted, she had cried most of that night and for days afterward. The memories still hurt and she didn't want to ever go through that pain again.

After their breakup Nick didn't try to call and she didn't want to talk to him. Then she discovered she was pregnant. Hurting, still angry with him, she'd planned to tell him about her pregnancy, but it was easier to keep quiet and avoid another confrontation. Nick would only push harder for marriage. He'd have to, as an out-of-wedlock baby would hurt his political future.

While she was thinking about how to tell him she was pregnant and what she would do about it in the future, time slipped past. From a friend she heard that Nick had gotten engaged. Shocked and angry with him, she was hurt badly that he had rushed into marriage with someone else so soon after breaking up with her. She'd decided to keep quiet about his child. He would marry and have his own family, and he didn't need to know about the baby she carried. Nick had made his choice, so she would go on with her life just as he had gone on with his.

Until now. Now he had lost his wife and their unborn child. For the first time since she had learned of her pregnancy she felt compelled to tell Nick about his son. In spite of the angry words, hurt feelings, the bitterness and heartbreak between them when they parted, she had to let him know he had a child. How they would work out sharing a son, she didn't know. But she knew it wasn't right to keep his son a secret when Nick had already lost one child.

Standing, she retrieved her phone and called home, wanting desperately to talk to Cody. Her grandmother answered and Claire felt like a child again, wanting to blurt out her problem and have her support and her wisdom. But she was grown now and she tried to shelter her grandmother from worries instead of taking them home to her. Grandma would have to know about this soon enough, but she didn't have to hear about it while Claire was halfway across the state of Texas.

She asked to talk to Cody. Just hearing his voice, she wished she could reach through the phone and hug him.

She talked to him about bugs and his fish tank—his two favorite topics. Then she talked briefly to Irene, his nanny, who was there two days a week and whenever Claire left town. She talked again to her grandmother, for almost an hour before she finally told them goodbye. When she ended the call, she burst into tears. The reality of her situation was too much to bear. Nick was so close to his dad, so tied into his own family, that she was certain he would want his son in his life. She would have to share Cody with Nick. But how?

For a long time she had tried to avoid thinking about Nick, but seeing him today, realizing she would have to bring him into her life and her family's lives, she could not keep him out of her thoughts. Staring into space, memories overwhelmed her.

A fellow Texan, Nick was in DC when she met him. She had graduated from college with a business degree and gone to work with her grandfather in his real estate business where she had worked part-time for years. When he sent her to Washington to a sales workshop, she had accepted a friend's invitation to a cocktail party. She remembered holding a martini that she hadn't even sipped when she looked across the room into the blue eyes of a tall, brown-haired man who gazed back. That first moment had been sizzling, a look that caught and held her attention.

As she gazed at him, he raised his glass as if in a toast and she couldn't keep from smiling and raising hers in return.

She had turned back to her new friend from Dallas. "See the brown-haired guy across the room? Do you know who he is?"

"Oh, yes. That's Nick Milan, a lawyer with a prestigious firm here. Rumor has it he'll be entering Texas politics someday. The Milans are a prominent old Texas family. Very wealthy." She sucked in a breath and grabbed her drink. "He's coming this way. I don't think it's to talk to me. I'll see you in a little while."

"Don't go. I don't even know him."

"You're going to," her friend replied, and moved away only seconds before Nick stepped in front of her.

Claire's heartbeat had sped up as she looked into the bluest eyes she'd ever seen.

"I think it's time we make our escape from this party. I'm Nick Milan, single and a lawyer. I live in Georgetown and I want to have dinner with you. And you are...?"

"Claire Prentiss. You use the fewest words and get to the point faster than any lawyer I have ever met," she said. "You don't even know if I have a husband here tonight."

"You don't have a wedding ring on your finger. I looked when I got close. If you had, I would have gone in another direction. May I take you to dinner?"

"That's nice, thank you, but you're a stranger. I usually know the people I go out with."

"You should be cautious, but this is an exception. First, I assure you I'm perfectly safe. Second, you can't deny we have chemistry between us. So go out with me."

She smiled. "Not too bashful, are you?"

He shrugged. "I know what I want." He set his drink down on a high-top table and speared her with his undivided attention. "If you need more information, I can tell you this. I'm from Dallas, where my dad's a judge, but I work in DC for Abrams, Wiesman and Wooten. Excellent client list, I might add." He nodded to where her friend had gone. "I saw you talking to Jen West. She's met me and knows who I am. She can vouch for my character. Or we can go find Lydia and she'll tell you more about me. Then we can tell her goodbye."

His fingers closed lightly on her arm and Claire walked with him to their slender, auburn-haired hostess, who turned to smile at them. "I see you two have met."

"Just met, Lydia," Nick said. "I need a character reference so I can talk Claire into going to dinner with me." He flashed Claire a smile that sent another sizzle through her.

"Now, do I want to give you that character reference or not?" Lydia teased.

"I think you just did," Claire replied. She turned to Nick. "I accept your offer. You can tell me all about yourself over dinner."

"Oh, my," Lydia said. "Now he won't stop talking until midnight."

"I promise, I will," he said to Claire, causing her to laugh again. "Lydia, we have to run. The party was delightful. Thank you so much for inviting me."

Claire also thanked Lydia and in seconds she was in a cab with Nick. She barely saw the elegant private club where he took her to dinner and she tasted only bites of a delicious, perfectly cooked sirloin. It was Nick who captivated her.

Tall, incredibly handsome and charismatic, he charmed her. She learned about his family, which had settled in Texas in the 1800s, mutual friends they had, Nick's political ambitions. She fell in love with Nick Milan that night.

When he asked her to come back to his place for a drink before he took her to her hotel, she agreed. The minute she walked through the entryway into the spacious living area in the suite on the thirty-third floor, she forgot the view and turned as Nick drew her into his embrace.

"This has been the perfect evening," he said. "I knew when I looked across the room and saw you that I wanted to get to know you and wanted to go out with you tonight," he said, his gaze going to her mouth.

She had stood on tiptoe, slipping her arms around his shoulders as he leaned down to kiss her. The moment his mouth touched hers, she was in flames. The chemistry between them had sparked and heated her all evening, but when he kissed her, desire consumed her.

They had made love that night and Nick had talked her into staying two extra days over the weekend.

He had finally called a cab to take her to the airport and, while they waited, he said he would fly to Houston the following weekend and meet her family. On weekends, over the next few months after their meeting in March, Nick had flown to Houston or she flew to DC. In June, on a weekend in Houston, Nick proposed marriage.

It had been a dream come true. She still remembered that night as if it had happened yesterday, not four years ago.

Attempting to shake off the mental picture of that night, Claire stood and walked to the window to gaze at the Dallas skyline. But she saw none of it because she was lost in memories. No matter how many times she thought of Nick's proposal, she always returned to the same answer—she could not leave her family.

When she had rejected his proposal, their fight had been bitter, deep and long-lasting. Nick had flown back to DC that night and they'd had no contact since. Nick had truly broken her heart, but if she had it to do over again she still wouldn't change her answer to him. She had done the only thing she could.

Whatever happened when she let him know about his son, she knew one thing: she'd never fall in love with him again because she never wanted to repeat that pain. And there was so much more to work out now between them, because Nick's political life was on a fast track, while she had her grandfather's business to run and still had her grandparents with her. Plus, the biggest issue of all, now they had a son and had to work out sharing him.

She caught her reflection in the window and saw the concern etched across her face and darkening her eyes. She turned away from the window. What she'd like to do right now was cancel their dinner date and fly home and never see Nick again, because whatever she did tonight, if she told him about his son, she would be hurt.

Nick's November wedding had been months before Cody's birth the following February. Claire had decided he would have his wife and someday, their children, so there was no need to even let him know about Cody.

Tonight, though, she had to tell him. Would he understand why she hadn't let him know? Nick was a successful, billionaire attorney from a family who had influential friends all over Texas. Would he want this son in his life after losing the baby he had expected?

He had been friendly today, but not the sexy guy who had flirted outrageously when he'd first met her and made it clear that he wanted to be with her. She felt he had asked her to dinner tonight on an impulse. Truthfully, if he hadn't been widowed, she would have turned him down. She'd had every intention of refusing his offer until she learned about the death of his wife and his unborn baby.

Glancing in the mirror of her dresser, she studied her business suit. Except for casual slacks and a cotton shirt for travel, this suit was all she had brought to wear and she had worn it all afternoon with Nick. Shedding the jacket, she picked up her purse and went downstairs. The hotel, she remembered, was close to an elegant boutique and she hurried, wanting to find a dress for tonight. If she had to tell Nick about Cody, she wanted to look her best when she did so.

At ten to seven, when she was finally ready, she stood in front of the same mirror to take one last look at herself.

She wore a pearl necklace given to her by her grand-father and a delicate pearl bracelet she had bought her-self. She turned slightly to look at her image, smoothing the flawless deep-blue long-sleeved dress with a plung-ing V neckline. Would Nick even notice her new dress? The Nick she had once known would, but she no longer knew this man.

There was only one way to find out, she told herself. She picked up her flat bag with her phone that held pictures of Cody, locked the door and left her hotel room.

As she rode down in an empty elevator, she couldn't shake the feeling of calamity. She couldn't get rid of her fear about Nick's reaction to the news she was about to tell him. Sure, she was afraid he'd be furious with her for keeping the secret. But far greater was her concern that Nick would want Cody in his life. He was a family man, close to his own father, so she was certain he and his par-ents would want to bring Cody into their family. The big question was, how much?

When she stepped off the elevator and gazed around the elegant lobby with its marble floor and potted palms, she spotted Nick instantly. In his charcoal suit and match-ing tie, he was definitely the most handsome man there. Crossing the expanse, he approached her.

Her heartbeat quickened, an unwanted reaction she

couldn't shake. She had a feeling she was in for another terrible fight with Nick and she didn't want to find him appealing at the same time. She wasn't going to let him hurt her again.

Trying to ignore the heat that enveloped her, she smiled at him and gripped her purse even more tightly. She had to get through this evening—without tears, without anger… and without desire. She took a deep breath and faced him. She had to. For Cody.

Two

As Nick watched Claire step off the elevator, desire surged in him. His gaze raked over her, taking in the low-cut blue dress that hugged her slender figure, revealed enticing curves, and ended high enough to display her long, shapely legs. Willowy and tall at five foot ten, she'd always worn clothes well. But there was something about her now...she was downright stunning.

He walked up to her. "Hi. You look great."

"Thank you." She nodded at him, then angled her head toward a corridor off the lobby. "The hotel has a great restaurant. We can eat here and it will be easier."

He smiled at her. "Taking you out to dinner is not a difficult task. C'mon," he said, ushering her toward the door. He'd already called the valet desk and had his car brought around to the front. As they crossed the lobby, he made small talk. "How's your family?"

"Mother passed away a little over a year ago and my

grandfather is in assisted living now. I hope he'll be able to return home before this year is over."

"I'm sorry to hear that. I guess your grandmother is in good health?"

"Yes, but she's older now and not quite the same. What about you? Do you enjoy being a State Representative?"

"Very much. Sometimes it's frustrating and occasionally it's disillusioning, but overall, I like politics and plan to run for a US Senate seat in the next election that will be four years from now."

"You're ambitious, but I knew that before. I'm sure you'd make a good senator, Nick."

"Thanks," he said, aware of her walking close beside him, catching a faint whiff of an exotic perfume he didn't recognize, but liked. He remembered how silky her hair had felt. In spite of their fiery split, he had never been able to forget her, yet there was no point in trying to see her after tonight. They would have the same difficulties, only now much more so, and he wasn't going to get hurt by her again.

When they exited the hotel, the valet opened the car door for her and she slid inside with a flash of her long legs that the valet admired as much as Nick did. He walked around to the driver's side, tipped the valet and thanked him for holding the door.

They drove out of the hotel's circular drive and in seconds were on the freeway. The winter sun had already set behind the tall buildings and the darkness was the perfect backdrop for the bright Christmas lights that gave a festive feeling to the night.

"Where are we going?" she asked, her question breaking the silence that had descended in the car.

"I'm taking you to a private club I belong to. It's quiet enough to talk and they have dancing on certain nights, more often now that it's December and there are more

Christmas parties," Nick said. "We can dance a few times, if I haven't forgotten how. I don't go out except with family or for business."

Her eyes widened as she turned to look at him. "That surprises you," he said.

"Yes. Somehow I pegged you for the type to sort of bounce back, if one ever can from that deep a loss."

"I guess I'm not," he replied abruptly. He didn't want to talk about that loss. His late wife and the child he'd never known were subjects best left for another time. If they had another time. Changing topics, he said, "The deal went smoothly today. Do you do much business in Dallas?"

"Very little," she replied. "We did this as a favor to a long-time client who suddenly went into the hospital and couldn't possibly come."

"Are you running the agency?"

"Yes, I am. They're giving Grandpa physical therapy and he hopes to regain his strength, but he can't ever be in charge again. Still, he can come to the office and be part of it, and that expectation keeps him going. One nice thing that made him happy—the agency has grown since I took over."

"That's what counts," Nick said. He wasn't surprised by her success. He'd always known she would be competent in running the agency and in dealing with people.

Soon he turned into well-tended grounds, winding through trees strung with miniature multicolored lights until they came to a sprawling stone building. Leaving his car with the valet, they entered the lobby where a huge Christmas tree stood in the center, and red ribbon and bows had been artfully strung along a hallway. Nick led her through the clubhouse to the dining room where they were seated at a corner table beside floor-to-ceiling windows that afforded a panoramic view of a golf course. More

Christmas lights lit up the covered veranda and, beyond that, a pond that held two fountains.

In one corner of the dining room a man played a ballad on a piano while two couples danced. The waiter came to take their orders and Nick asked for white wine. When it was poured, he raised his glass. "Here's to a successful deal that closed easily today."

"I'll drink to that, Nick," she said solemnly, her dark eyes filled with unfathomable secrets. He wondered about her life now. For all she'd said so far, she'd told him nothing except that she was head of the family real estate agency.

"Let's see if I've forgotten how to dance," he said, standing, curious if she would dance with him. She was cool, standoffish and seemed preoccupied tonight. He wondered whether she was worried about her grandfather or if something else was disturbing her. Or was it a lasting anger with him over their breakup? She wasn't the light-hearted, fun-filled Claire he had known, but he wasn't the same person anymore, either.

They went to the dance floor where he put his hand on her waist, careful to keep distance between them as they danced to a soft ballad. "You're not out of practice," he said, remembering other times they'd danced together, him holding her close, his heart racing. Even now, he had a sharp awareness of her as she gazed at him intently.

"You're not out of practice either, Nick." He accepted her compliment. "You know, if you're so steeped in politics, I imagine you are out and about plenty."

"Usually at stuffy dinners or fund-raisers. Not much time to find a pretty woman and dance at those events."

He wasn't sure but he thought he saw her cheeks blush before she turned her head. He pulled her slightly closer and gave himself over to the dance. He liked the sensation of having her in his arms. She felt good. Familiar. From out of the blue, one thought kept reverberating in his head. *This woman could have been your wife.*

He still felt heartache thinking about what could have been.

Four years ago when Claire had turned down his marriage proposal and he returned to Washington, he'd turned to Karen. They had dated in college and law school, and known each other since high school, so their relationship seemed only natural once she'd accepted a job in DC working in the office of a friend of her father's.

Nick couldn't work things out with Claire and Karen was there, in DC, wanting to go out, charming him and filling a big void. She was from Dallas, their parents were friends and she would live wherever he wanted. She had wanted marriage. His firm wanted their young attorneys married and so did his parents. He still loved Claire but he knew it was over between them.

Doing what his family, his firm and his career indicated he should, he had proposed to Karen. He could still remember a moment at his wedding when he had been hit by a wall of longing, knowing that it should have been Claire beside him, but he had banked those feelings. Karen had been a good wife, seductive and beautiful, and he had grown to appreciate her more each year. She catered to him, bolstered his career, moved with him, and in return he gave her the social life she wanted. Both sets of parents were happy. Claire was out of his life.

But he had never forgotten her.

Even now, as he danced with her, he had to remind himself that there wasn't any point in trying to see her again after tonight. She was tied to her family and to Houston more than ever, while he had his life in Dallas and DC and he had a political career that held golden promises for the future.

What about the sizzling current he felt as they danced? There was no denying she still had a physical effect on him, but that might simply be because he had been alone for so long now.

As he spun her around and dipped her in time to the music, he was swept away by vivid memories of holding her tightly, kissing her, making love to her. For an instant desire flashed, hot and unwanted, as he looked down at her mouth, wanting to hold her close, feel her softness while he kissed her. He remembered how soft and sweet her lips had been, and more than anything he wanted to taste them again. The desire was undeniable. Lust slammed into him, rising to the surface and surprising him after two long years of total numbness.

But he wouldn't kiss her.

He couldn't.

He swung her up to continue dancing, trying to cool down, to forget the scalding memories. There was no future in seeing Claire and he would not start that again.

Trying to divert his mind from taking her right there on the dance floor, he began questioning her. "Who's the man in your life, Claire?" he asked, certain there had to be one.

She shook her head. "There isn't one. No time. I'm too busy running the office, making sales myself, taking care of my family, visiting Grandpa five days a week. I don't have a social life except through the office, church and family. I keep thinking it will change and things will settle down, but that hasn't happened."

"Maybe you're working too hard. How big is your agency?" He was grateful for the safe path the conversation now took.

"I have three offices and almost seventy salespeople. We deal in commercial and residential properties."

"That's a big business," he said. Studying her, Nick

guessed she was tied into work most of her waking hours. "How many offices did you have when your grandfather turned things over to you? I thought there was only one."

"One is correct," she replied. "Good memory, Nick. I've been very lucky and have some great people who work for me."

"I imagine luck is only a part of it. Congratulations. I'm impressed," he said, meaning it. "You have to be a busy woman."

"I am busy. And I've got a full day tomorrow. I'm flying home at six in the morning. Have to be at the airport at four because I'm not one to run out there at the last minute."

"I'll take you to the airport."

She laughed, her eyes suddenly twinkling, stirring another flash of desire as he remembered the fun he once had with her. "Thanks, Nick, but that's beyond the call of 'for old times' sake.' I already have a limo reserved. Thanks, anyway. That's very nice of you."

"If you change your mind, the offer stands."

The number ended and a fast one started. As they danced and he watched her hips move, he was assailed by memories once again. He couldn't help remembering making love with her. He couldn't help wanting her now, which shocked him again. He had a reaction to Claire that he hadn't had to any other woman since Karen. Maybe it was time for him to come back into the world. Yet, even as he thought that, he knew he didn't want to get involved with any woman at this time in his life. Definitely not Claire. He'd been there and done that and gotten hurt badly.

Trying to stop watching Claire so closely and shutting down the erotic images in his memory, he was grateful when the song ended. "Ready to sit one out? I'd like a sip of wine." They returned to the table.

They talked through their dinners—steak for him and

salmon for her, which he noticed she barely ate. She had to be worried about something at home, her family or business, because she seemed preoccupied. He felt a wall between them, but he didn't particularly care. After a polite goodbye, he wouldn't see her again, so it didn't matter.

If she had said she was seeing someone, he would have not been surprised. The invisible barrier between them kept her restrained, as if she had accepted his invitation tonight to be polite and she would be glad to tell him goodbye. Two or three times he had caught her looking at him with an intensity that startled him. Was she still thinking about their last angry moments together? Each time she had quickly looked away, her face had flushed. So there was something disturbing her, keeping a wall up...

Was it him? But that was impossible, unless she was still hurting from their breakup. But he couldn't imagine that she hadn't gone on with her life. Or was it—

No. He had to stop attempting to figure out what she might be thinking. Soon she would be out of his life again, this time probably for good.

She may have been thinking the same thing, because she put down her coffee cup and said, "Nick, it's been interesting to see you and I know it's not late, but I have an early flight."

"Sure," he said, picking up on her need to leave. He signed for the check and led her out, telling himself it was for the best. But he couldn't help the disappointment that he never would know the reason for those intense looks.

As Nick drove her back to the hotel, Claire rehearsed asking him to come in for a few minutes. She knew that, being the gentleman he was, he would see her to her door. Once there, it would be so simple to invite him in. But there would be nothing simple about confessing to him she had given birth to his son. Informing him that he had a three-year-old son was not the sort of thing to tell him over dinner in a public place. She had to be alone with him and her last opportunity was approaching.

At the hotel, he gave his car to the valet, saying he'd be right back.

She shivered as they walked into the lobby, blaming the chilly evening air. As they rode up in the elevator and walked to her door, her stomach was in knots and she dreaded breaking the news to him. Nick still seemed wrapped in mourning for his wife, but the fact that he had lost his unborn child made it imperative to inform him of his son.

She couldn't look back and wish she had told him long ago because that was over and done. Maybe she should take a few days to think things through before she told him about Cody. She hadn't had time to really consider how the situation was going to change her life and Cody's life permanently. Not to mention Nick's life, too.

"Claire, is something wrong?"

His voice cut into her reverie and she started, realizing she was still standing in front of her hotel room door, the key card in her hand.

He'd given her the perfect opening...except the words wouldn't come. Even though she was freezing, perspiration broke out on her forehead and her palms grew damp.

Tell him. Tell him now.

But she couldn't.

"No, I just got to thinking about something that has become a problem in my life," she said.

"Maybe you're working too hard," Nick said quietly, running his finger along her cheek.

She looked up into those deep blue eyes with thick lashes, into Nick's handsome face. Nick was a good person, intelligent, sophisticated, reasonable, charming. She should just tell him about his son. At the same time, she recalled the bitter accusations they had flung at each other when they had parted—she'd called him a selfish rich guy who always got what he wanted, while he'd accused her of not having a life of her own.

If she told him about his son, what hurtful things would they say to each other tonight? She didn't want to go through that kind of stormy battle with Nick again.

"Nick—" She paused. The moment she told him, Cody would no longer belong to her side of the family only. She would have to share him and let him stay with Nick. Or worse. Would Nick try to take Cody from her?

"Yes?" Nick prompted, curiosity in his expression.

"I had a really good time tonight," she said softly, barely able to get out the words.

He tilted his head to look intently at her again. "I'm glad. I wasn't sure you were having that much fun. It was a good evening for me. How about a kiss for old times' sake?" he said and leaned down to place his mouth lightly on hers while his arm circled her waist.

The moment his mouth touched hers, she felt the sparks she always had with Nick. His arm tightened around her waist and his mouth pressed against hers more firmly, opening her lips as he really kissed her, a deep, sexy kiss that for a few minutes stopped her worrying and fears, and shut off memories of their past and the big problem facing her.

Her heart pounding, she clung to Nick and kissed him in return, knowing it was folly, but unable to stop. She was swept back in time, into memories of Nick's steamy, passionate kisses that had stolen her heart so quickly. She ignored the voice in her head that warned her she couldn't let that happen again.

She clung to his broad shoulders, too aware of the hard,

muscled body pressed against hers. Desire seemed to explode from his scalding kiss. It had been so long since she had been held by a man and kissed with such intensity.

When they moved apart, he was breathing as hard as she and he looked startled. His kiss had shaken her, igniting desire that burned through worry and made her stop thinking for a few minutes. But now, as she faced him again, she saw his blue eyes were filled with curiosity. Nick was an intelligent man and he had already picked up on something worrying her.

She couldn't tell him. The words wouldn't come to invite him in. She could take a few days to think about what she intended to do and to consult her family lawyer. She smiled at him, trying to pull herself together. "Thank you for the wonderful dinner, Nick. It was good to see you again. I am so sorry about your wife and baby."

"You're saying all the right things, Claire, but why do I have a feeling there is something else you want to say?" he asked, studying her as if he hadn't ever seen her before.

"No, Nick. I'm just overworked at home." Nervous, wanting to get away from him, swamped in guilt at the same time, she inserted her card into the door with such a shaky hand, she couldn't get it to work.

Nick's hand closed over hers and he opened the door for her. Even in her upset condition, she noticed the physical contact, the warmth of his fingers that sent an electric charge up her arm with his touch. "If you ever want to talk, I'm an old friend, Claire," he said quietly.

She felt as if she had fallen into ice water. "Thank you. Good night, Nick," she said, stepping inside and holding the door, turning to look at him. "I'll keep that in mind."

He nodded, giving her one more searching look before walking to the elevator.

She started to close the door and guilt swamped her.

Could she live with her conscience if she flew home to Houston and didn't tell Nick?

Closing her eyes, she opened the door just as the elevator doors opened. Nick glanced over his shoulder, saw her watching him and frowned.

"Nick, can you come in for a little while?"

He turned, once again giving her one of his probing looks that filled her with dread. Nick could be formidable. He had power, wealth and a state-wide network of cronies with influence. What would he do when he found out about Cody?

"Claire, I'll be happy to help with a problem," he said in a gentle voice, but it did nothing to ease her fear.

"Come in and let's get a drink," she said, leading him into the living area of her suite, which overlooked the sparkling lights of the city from the twenty-fourth floor. She switched on one small lamp that gave a soft glow in the quiet room. "I'm trying to think things through before I start talking. Just give me a minute," she said. "What would you like?"

"Let's see if there's any beer in that fridge you have," he said. Looking in the small refrigerator, he held up a bottle of white wine. "Would you like this?"

"Yes, thank you," she said.

"I'll pour your wine. You go ahead and think so we can talk. I'm in no hurry, Claire."

She nodded and he went to pour her wine, but as she watched him walk away, she knew she couldn't think this through in just minutes. She got her phone out of her purse, still half wanting to tell him to forget it and talk to him later, by phone from Houston. Each time she had thoughts like that, guilt chased them away. She couldn't fly home without telling Nick that he had a child.

Perching on the edge of an ottoman, she watched him

stroll back into the room. She couldn't have chosen better for the father of her child. Nick had so many good qualities. She hoped forgiveness was one of them.

He handed her a glass of white wine. When his fingers brushed hers, he frowned slightly. "You're freezing," he said, his hand covering hers. His hand was warm and in other circumstances would have been reassuring. But not now. He knelt in front of her. "What's wrong? It can't be money with the successful business you have. Are you not well?"

She shook her head, unable to say anything.

"How can I help?" he asked gently.

"I want to talk to you. Have a seat, Nick. This may take a while."

His probing gaze searched hers again before he rose, pulled a straight-back chair close and sat. She sipped her wine and set the glass on an end table. When she did, he took her hand, holding it between his two warm hands.

"Do you want me to get you a blanket?"

"No, I'll be all right." They gazed at each other and she realized he was being quiet to give her a chance to think and to let her talk when she was ready.

"Nick, the night you proposed…we had a terrible fight and you said goodbye. You walked out and we didn't see each other again. It wasn't many months until you were engaged to someone else and headed for a political career. I'm sure you remember."

"Of course I do. We couldn't work things out." He took a swallow of his beer, as if to wash away the memory of their breakup. "Karen and I had known each other for years and we'd dated in college and at one point had talked about marriage. When she came to work in DC she called me and I started seeing her. She was from Dallas, had no ties that would interfere with the two of us. My family pushed me to marry and start a family. You had already turned me down. That last time you and I were together…it was terrible. I imagine you were as hurt as I was. It was clear that it was over between us."

She nodded her head, giving him the affirmation he was looking for. Then he continued.

"I proposed to Karen and she accepted. I know it was fast and I know I should have called to let you know so you heard it from me, but…well, I didn't think you'd want to hear from me at all."

"I heard you were dating and then I heard you were engaged. I was shocked, but I understood that we couldn't work out our problems. You had your life in politics and in DC at the time, working at that well-known law firm. It was obvious you would be successful and you were ambitious. The hurtful words we had finally ended it between us. I let you go out of my life and I knew eventually you would have your own life, your wife, your family."

"That's what I planned," he said quietly, looking down at the beer in his hand and then taking a drink before he lowered it to look at her and wait for her to speak.

"We had really gone our separate ways and you were starting a new life."

"What you want to tell me—does it have something to do with me?" he asked, sounding puzzled.

She nodded. "I just want you to remember that you had your own life planned, a new career, a future in politics, a new wife. You lived in your world."

She could see she had his full attention and she was certain he was trying to figure out how anything in her life could involve him. She took a deep breath and hoped she wasn't making the biggest mistake of her life.

"Nick, at that time I was pregnant with your son."

Three

Stunned, Nick could only stare at her as he tried to register her words. "That was almost four years ago," he whispered, talking more to himself than to her. She couldn't have had his baby. He gazed into her big, dark-brown eyes that still hid secrets and saw her wring her hands. She looked pale, afraid, her shoulders slightly hunched. She was telling him the truth. Four years ago he had gotten her pregnant. Nine months later, she had given birth to his baby and hadn't told him.

He had a son. He would have to be three now. Nick was so stunned he couldn't breathe. He couldn't believe that he was a dad. Gulping for breath, he stood and walked to the window. Like shock waves that kept hitting him, the realization rocked him again that he was a dad, he had a son, a child of his own. He turned to look at Claire.

"Dammit, Claire. I have a child and you didn't tell me," he said, clenching his fists and shaking, anger and shock jolting him. "How could you not tell me? Dammit," he snapped, without giving her time to answer.

He could only stare at her and think back. He had been in love with her, had proposed to her and wanted to marry her. And then they'd fought. On the rebound he had married Karen. He hadn't talked to Claire again and she hadn't talked to him—a natural outcome of the last hours of arguing, flinging accusations, letting a wall of anger and hurt come between them.

And now to learn that he had a son and Claire had never told him shocked and angered him all over again. He placed his hands on his hips without thinking what he was doing. "You never intended to tell me. The only reason you did is because we saw each other today," he said, fury beginning to boil.

She stood and faced him. "When you told me you had lost your wife and unborn baby, I realized you had to be told. Before, an out-of-wedlock baby would have hurt or ruined your political aspirations and you know it. You wouldn't have wanted to hear from me. When you married, I always thought you would have your family with your wife and you really would never be that interested in a child I carried."

"My son? Of course, I would be interested. I have a son," he said, feeling awe. "Claire, that is the most fantastic news I could possibly hear. How in hell could you think I wouldn't be interested?"

"I just told you—news that I had given birth to your son just after your marriage would have killed your political career. You married within months after our breakup. I wondered if you had been seeing her while you were seeing me. Your new wife certainly would not have wanted to hear that I had your baby." Claire closed her eyes and swayed, and he frowned, wondering whether she was about to faint. "Nick, can't you see that I felt you shut me out of your life? Without telling me anything you became engaged. You should have let me know."

"I should have done that, I agree."

"Recriminations aren't going to help. I'm just trying to explain my actions."

"You can't ever explain not letting me know," he said.

"I just did. Would you have wanted to tell your fiancée you had recently gotten me pregnant? You married and occasionally I saw pictures in the news of you with your wife and you looked happy. Why would I think you would want my baby just when you married Karen?"

Knowing she was right, he didn't care. The knowledge that he had a son was far more important.

"I've missed all his first years. I missed his babyhood. He doesn't know me. He doesn't even know I exist, does he?"

"No, he's little."

"Dammit, Claire, I've missed too much."

"Hindsight is always better," she replied, looking pained. "I've told you why I did what I did. It's that simple. But I will say this. This son is not going to help your political life, I promise you."

"I don't give a damn about that. It's far more important that I know my son."

"You say that now, but you don't really mean it. Your adult life has revolved around politics and rising to the next office," she said.

"I mean it, Claire. My son is my future, not a job. You can't keep me from getting to know him."

"I don't plan to, Nick. That's why I've told you about him." She glanced away. "But your family will not be happy, especially your father. You know he would not have been happy to hear about a child—not then and not now."

Nick inhaled and clenched his fists, trying to hang on to his temper. "You took those years from me, and I can never get them back."

She wiped the tears from her eyes. "I regret that now."

"I've been through hell the past two years. I lost my wife and baby. I could have filled part of that void and helped the hurt by knowing my son. I can't believe you did this to me."

She looked at him. "Nick, I'm so sorry for your loss and if I had known—" She bit off her words and wrung her hands. "I wish I could undo the past few years, but I can't. We'll have to pick up from here."

"Dammit, Claire," he said, clenching his fists and closing his eyes. Hurting, he thought of all the empty moments. He'd hurt badly after the breakup with Claire. Two years ago, he'd hurt after losing Karen and the baby. Now he had another deep hurt and this one could have been so easily avoided. He tried to hang on to his temper and to avoid saying hurtful things to Claire because it really didn't help to pour out his fury on her.

"Would you like to see his picture?" she asked after a few minutes.

Nick jerked his head up. His anger melted as fast as it had come and awe filled him. He suddenly knew how he would have felt if he had been present at the birth of his son. "You have his picture? Of course I'd like to see it."

She walked back to the ottoman to pick up her phone. Nick came to stand beside her. "I named him Cody Nicholas Prentiss."

"You named him Nicholas?" he asked, pleasure filling him.

"Yes. I named him for you," she said, looking up at him. "I felt I should do that."

Nick looked at her phone and she opened it, handing it

to him. His hands shook and he was overwhelmed as he looked at a child that resembled his own pictures when he was small.

"Oh, my word, there's no doubt about his heritage. He looks just like me at that age," Nick said, the feeling of awe swamping him. "My family will love him beyond words. Thank you for naming him Nicholas."

"He looks like you. He's a sweet, happy little boy who loves people. Even as a baby, he smiled constantly when someone talked to him."

"That's great," Nick said, still staring at Cody's picture.

"My grandmother watches him a couple of days a week, and I have a nanny the rest of the time to help relieve Grandma. For his first seven months I took maternity leave. Grandpa was around until the past six months, so there was a man in the house."

Looking at his son, Nick felt the sting of tears of joy, forgetting his anger and the empty years. Getting a grip on his emotions, he wiped his eyes. "I have a son," he said, his voice filled with awe. "This is the most wonderful news. Claire, he's perfect. Was your family with you when he was born?" he asked, staring at Cody's picture.

"Oh, yes. Mom was alive then, and all of them were thrilled. When he was a baby, one of us rocked him to sleep every night. Grandpa read to him when he was so tiny he couldn't possibly understand a word, but it made him happy."

"Can you send this picture to me?"

"Yes. I have more on my iPad. I'll go get it. I'll send all of them to you," she said.

Nick watched her leave the room, his gaze sweeping down to notice her tiny waist, the slightest sway to her walk, her long legs. What if they had married? What if he had tried harder to work things out with her? He had been so in love with her, but their breakup had been final. Then Karen had come along and she seemed to be the answer to his problems. In their marriage they'd each gotten what they'd wanted. But even as he had walked down the aisle, his heart had ached. He'd tried to remind himself that Claire didn't want to marry him, but that hadn't stopped the hurt that had torn him up for a long time.

If he had known about her pregnancy—

Instantly he stopped that thought. There was no undoing the past and he wasn't going to dwell on what might have been.

As Claire left the room, he stared at the empty doorway. Fury still simmered in him because of the years he had missed with his son. At the same time, awe and joy were stronger. This couldn't bring back the baby he had lost, but Cody would fill a painful void in his life.

Staring at the picture, memorizing it, he held her phone in his hands. It was incredibly awesome to look at the picture and see a child who looked just like he had when he was that age. How long would it take to get used to Claire's revelation?

"Cody Nicholas," he whispered, running his fingers over the picture.

She came back into the room with her iPad in hand and motioned to the sofa. Again, he watched her cross the room. Her attention was on her tablet and his gaze ran from her head to her toes. His pulse raced as he looked at her. She was stunning, even better looking than she had been four years ago. Today she had been poised, self-assured, handling the business matters with ease and he'd admired her. Tonight he had seen the sexy side of her and he'd still responded to her. Now he discovered she was the mother of his baby and he was shocked.

Each time he thought about this discovery, joy, awe and

gratitude outweighed anger. He should do something to show her how happy he was and he should try to forgive her. The latter would take some time, but Claire was the mother of his child and he needed to keep that in mind.

"Come sit and I'll show you his pictures," she said, still focused on the iPad in her hands, but she sounded more like herself. "I have baby pictures on here."

"Thank heavens for that," he said. He caught her before she sat and grasped her gently by the shoulders.

Wide-eyed, she looked up. "What?"

"You're the mother of my child, Claire. We have a tie now for the rest of our lives. Even though I can't help being angry, I'm far more thrilled and grateful. I'm sorry I wasn't there for you, but that was your choosing. One thing is important for me to say. Thank you. Even though it's completely inadequate."

Wrapping his arms around her, he hugged her to him. "Thank you," he said again, his words muffled this time. She was warm, soft in his arms. It was suddenly so good to hold her. "Thank you," he repeated, a knot in his throat. They stood in silence a moment until he felt tears on his neck and leaned away.

He stroked the moisture away with his fingers. "Why are you crying?"

"Don't take him from me, Nick," she whispered, her eyes shut tightly as she wiped at her cheeks. "I know you'll want him in your life. Your parents will, too, after they meet him."

Nick folded her into his embrace again and held her close. He wasn't making any promises because he didn't know what demands she would have. He framed her face with his hands. "I don't know what we'll work out, but I will never take him totally away from you. That would be harming my own child."

Nodding, she moved away, turning her back to dry her eyes, and he wondered whether she even believed what he said.

"Let's see his pictures," Nick said. He sat beside her on the sofa and she gave him the iPad. He pulled up photos and she tapped one.

"We'll start when he was a tiny baby. This is in the hospital."

"Send these to me, all of them. Oh, hell, why didn't you let me know?" he asked, hurting as he looked at a sleeping newborn with a blue cap on his head.

"I've already given you all my reasons. But let me ask you this. Would you have felt the same about Cody then?"

He gazed into her dark eyes and thought about what she'd asked. "I might not have felt this way right after getting married, and you're right. Karen probably would not have taken the news well, but I still think you should have told me. I missed this. Especially after losing Karen and the baby. I missed these years," he said, looking down at the date Claire had written on a picture of her and Cody as they left the hospital.

"Claire, this date—" He frowned. "I wasn't engaged when you found out you were pregnant. Not if you carried Cody nine months."

She raised her chin, gazing at him with a defiant expression. "I was shocked when I found out I was pregnant. I needed time to figure out my future and adjust to the realization I was going to have a baby. I had to tell my family. I was trying to plan what I would do when I heard you were engaged."

"It was early enough I might not have married Karen," he said, wondering what he would have done.

Claire rubbed her forehead. "We had already had that

terrible breakup. I don't see how we could have gotten back together."

"True," he said, staring into space, thinking about that time in his life. He glanced at the iPad on his knee. "Let's get back to the pictures," he said, turning to the next one, another of her leaving the hospital, carrying a small bundle in her arms. Cody was so wrapped in blankets he was not visible. In the next picture the blankets were peeled back so his face showed. He was sleeping and looked wonderful to Nick. "I've been cheated of having these years together with two of my babies," he said, anger surfacing again.

Nick looked at pictures of Cody in a baby bed, of him being held in Claire's arms and then being held by each member of her family. He looked at his son's nursery room with Winnie-the-Pooh characters painted on the wall.

"You weren't ever going to tell me about him, were you?" Even though he kept his voice quiet, Nick's anger escalated, wondering if he could ever be with her again without feeling anger over keeping his son from him. Would he ever trust her in anything?

"I knew I had to eventually. Cody would get bigger and want to know about his dad. I couldn't avoid it forever, but as time passed, it just got easier to let it go," she said quietly.

Nick held back an angry reply and looked at the next group of pictures as Cody grew and had his first birthday. Nick felt another pang of longing. "Where was his first birthday?"

"At my grandparents'. Now they live in my house. I had a home built and moved Grandma in with me."

They bent over each picture with Claire telling him about the incident when the picture was taken. He laughed as he looked at a picture of Cody with chocolate cake all over his small hands and across his face.

"This is great," Nick said, more to himself than her. "He looks as if he loves the cake and is having a wonderful time."

"He did. That was the first time he ever tasted chocolate. He still doesn't get any candy."

Nick turned to look at her. "With you and your grandparents hovering over him, and your mother, too, this first year, he was probably a very well cared for baby and a very happy one."

He turned his attention back to the pictures. In the next one Claire was in a swimsuit, holding Cody's hands as he waded in the shallow end of a large swimming pool.

"Whose pool is this?"

"A friend's. I don't want a pool while Cody is little, although he does actually know how to paddle across the pool and climb out, which is an enormous relief. It doesn't mean I don't watch him, but it's good to know that he can swim out if he falls in."

Nick's attention shifted from Cody to Claire's picture in a deep blue one-piece suit. "You don't look as if you've had a baby," he said, thinking she looked great. His gaze ran over the picture as he looked at her long, shapely legs, her tiny waist and full, luscious curves. He felt it again. Desire. Claire was making him come alive again, reminding him what it felt like to know lust. He glanced her way and suddenly felt the heat emanating from her body as she sat so close beside him. He wanted to hold her. But he knew he couldn't. Not now. With an effort he kept his hands to himself and focused again on the pictures.

She thanked him for the compliment. "I used to hit the gym three days a week. Now I have an exercise room at home."

"You're bound to go out with someone, Claire."

She shook her head. "I'm so busy, and when I do have

time, I spend it with Cody. I'd much rather be doing something with him. I take at least one day a week to work from home. Of course, that may change when he starts school, but it works for right now."

"I'm glad." Nick never had any doubt she'd be a good mother for his son, though he had to admit he was surprised that no man had snatched her up yet. Successful, beautiful and single—that should draw men easily. He suspected she must be sending them on their way, which gave him a stab of satisfaction that he dismissed as ridiculous.

"Was he an easy baby or difficult?"

"Oh, so easy, but remember—there were four adults living with him, three to care for him. Mom really couldn't, but she could talk to him and read to him and do things like that with him. We'd help her hold him. Anyway, that made his care easy and everyone was relaxed, so he probably relaxed. He's a sweetie."

"I want to meet him as soon as possible."

"We'll arrange it, Nick." As she looked at him, he gazed into the eyes that always hid what she felt. Big, beautiful brown eyes that made him want to slide his hand behind her head and draw her closer. "Nick, let me take your picture so I can show it to Cody when I get home and tell him about you."

He nodded. "Why don't we take a selfie and then we'll be in it together. I'd feel better about him seeing me with you."

She nodded.

Nick placed his arm around her. "I have longer arms—why don't I take the picture?"

"Go ahead," she said, and from the somber sound of her voice he wondered whether she would even smile. She sounded as if she was headed for disaster instead of just taking a picture with him. He held out the iPad. "Try to look happy, Claire. Think about Cody." Nick took their picture.

He pulled up the picture and smiled. "Thanks, Claire. That looks good."

"He'll want to see what you look like."

"That hasn't ever come up? He hasn't asked about a dad?"

"No. We don't talk about you and he isn't in school yet, so he isn't with other kids a lot."

"Doesn't he have any little friends?"

"Oh, sure, but they play. There isn't a lot of discussion. He's three, Nick. Besides, kids take things as they come."

Nick continued looking at pictures of Cody, of Claire or her family with Cody as he went from being a baby to a toddler.

"I can't wait to meet him," he said. "I can fly to Houston Friday, so can we spend time together this weekend?"

She ran her hand across her forehead. "I didn't even think this through when I told you tonight. I was so shocked today to learn about your loss that right then and there I decided I had to tell you about Cody. But I—I need time. I'll have to break the news to Cody."

"A child accepts life as it comes. You just said that. So he'll accept meeting me. Would you prefer to bring him to Dallas? I just want to meet him as soon as possible."

"It's a complete upheaval in all of our lives, including yours," she whispered, wringing her hands.

He nodded. "Not just meeting him."

She looked stricken and he tried to hang on to his patience. His request wasn't unreasonable in his opinion. Why couldn't she see that?

"All right. Do you want to come Friday night?"

He opened his phone, checked his calendar and nodded.

"Yes. After we meet, would he like it if I take everyone to dinner? This includes your grandmother, of course."

"That's nice, Nick." But as much as her words were gracious, he could hear her trepidation in her voice and see it in her eyes. She gazed up at him solemnly, with a touch of fear in their depths. He knew she was worried that she would have to give up her child permanently, yet he couldn't feel much sympathy for her since she had kept knowledge of his baby from him all this time.

Verifying his interpretation, she took a deep breath and said, "Nick, my grandma is elderly and frail now. Since Mom died, Cody and I and Grandpa are her whole world. She's older and vulnerable. Please, think of her before you take any action. She doesn't have that many years left."

"I will, Claire. I won't spring anything on you without discussing it." He paused a few minutes and silence fell. Finally, he asked, "Does Cody have a favorite place to eat?"

"We really don't get out a lot, but there's one place he loves—a restaurant made to look like a rainforest. He thinks it's very special and a lot of fun."

"I'll make reservations."

"He'll love it." She smiled. She'd been so worried, so tearful in the last while that her smile caught him off guard. He took a moment to look at her. She really was a beautiful woman, with her smooth skin and big, dark eyes fringed with thick lashes.

"Does he resemble you at all?"

"Not in looks, as you saw. Actually, probably not much in temperament, either. He has a ready smile the way you used to, and he's a little charmer and very social. If I take him to the office, he's all over the place talking to everyone and they talk to him."

Nick smiled. "I don't know that I was all that charming as a kid. I remember Wyatt and Madison constantly telling me to be still. I don't believe I charmed them." His older brother and sister had avoided him at all costs, just the way he did his younger brother Tony.

She gave him a faint smile. "Siblings are different."

He glanced at his watch. "You're not going to have much time to sleep before leaving for the airport."

"I wouldn't have slept anyway."

He nodded, suspecting he wasn't going to sleep in the hours he had left, either. "Claire, cancel your flight. I have a family plane and a pilot. I'll get him to fly you to Houston whenever you want. This way you won't have to wait for the commercial flight and maybe you'll have a little more time to yourself before going to the office."

She stared at him a moment and then nodded. "Thanks, Nick. I can't wait to see Cody."

"Neither can I, Claire," he said. She looked startled and drew a deep breath as if he had suggested something dreadful. There was no doubt that she regretted telling him. If his client hadn't asked him to the closing, would he ever have known about his son? That question persisted and each time stirred his anger because he wondered how old Cody would have been before she told him.

"I'll make arrangements for you to fly home. What time do you want to leave?"

"As soon as I can get to the airport," she replied.

He nodded. "I'll call my pilot while you cancel your flight."

By the time she returned he had made all the arrangements. "I have a limo picking us up in an hour," he told her. "If you need to pack, go ahead. In the meantime I'll look at Cody's pictures and send copies to myself. I can't seem to look enough. I just want to sit and stare at some of these pictures. He looks like the most adorable child I have ever seen in my entire life."

She gave him a fleeting smile. "I know exactly how you feel. He is a very handsome little boy, Nick."

"What does he like? He's too little to read."

"He knows his alphabet. My grandmother plays all kinds of letter games with him. He's a smart little boy. You'll be proud of him."

"I already love him with all my heart and I haven't even seen him," Nick said, looking up at her and seeing a wistful expression on her face that startled him. Was she wondering what it might have been like if they had been together? When she met his gaze, her expression changed, a shuttered look coming across her eyes that locked him out.

"Whatever we work out and whatever happens in the future, you've made me a very happy man tonight," he said.

Her dark gaze was unfathomable as she nodded. "I'm glad, Nick. It'll be good for Cody to know you. He has a very good man for a father."

"I hope I'm a good dad. I've had a good dad, although one who liked to run everything and goes too far sometimes. I'm in politics because of him, yet at the same time, he's been a big help to me. When the dust settles, they'll all be happy about Cody."

"Nick, take a moment to think before you announce that you have a son. You have such high political ambitions, and you have a career as a politician. Judge Milan is not going to be pleased. None of your close circle of supporters will be happy. An out-of-wedlock baby so close to your marriage isn't going to be good news to any of them. Your political career means everything to you, so you should give some thought to what you're about to do."

He nodded. "I'm not shutting my son out of my life because of politics. Right now, I get sympathy because of being a widower. That will help cushion this announcement. I want this senate seat and I think I can win. I told you when we dated that I want to be President someday, Claire. There are people already working on that in the background."

She stared at him. "A scandal could make that extremely difficult, unless we marry and that's over between us."

"If Cody kills my chances, so be it. At this point in my life I'm aeons away from the White House. I have to win the senate seat first."

"Your dad is going to push you to marry me. The kind of political career he wants you to have takes a lot of background work. He's already put a lot into your career."

He put up a hand to stop her argument. "Claire, we're not going to make any big decisions tonight. And right now I only want to talk about my son. What can I bring Cody that he would really like?"

"He likes his books. I'll text you a list to choose from. And he likes to build things. He likes electronic gadgets and he knows how to find some of his games on the computer." He could see how her eyes lit up again as she talked about her son. "I can't wait to see him. I've got to go pack. Look at his pictures and I'll get ready to go home."

She left the room and he continued sending himself each picture of Cody. In a short time Claire appeared with her carry-on, a briefcase and her purse. She had changed and wore the tailored navy skirt and the matching silk blouse she had worn to the closing. Once again he thought how good-looking she was, even more than she had been years ago, and he thought of his earlier kiss, which had rocked him and stirred desire.

"You look nice. You also travel lightly."

"It was just an overnight."

"The limo is downstairs if you're ready," he said, handing her iPad back, which she slipped into her purse.

"Yes. I'm checked out and ready to go," she said. Nick

shouldered her carry-on and picked up her briefcase while she slid her purse strap over her shoulder. They were ready to leave her hotel room, and for one brief moment, he wished he could pull her into his arms and kiss her again. Controlling the urge, he held the door for her, catching a whiff of her perfume as she walked out. It was the same scent she'd worn years ago, and as he inhaled it he was transported back in time.

He remembered his third flight to Houston to see her for the weekend. She had moved back home to help with her family, and her grandmother had ushered him inside. As he'd walked in, Claire came down the stairs. She had taken his breath away that night in a bright-red crepe dress that ended above her knees. Her thick hair swung loosely across her shoulders as she descended the steps and he could only stare, not hearing what her grandmother said.

Nick was so caught up in the memory that he didn't realize they had reached the airport until the limo slowed near the plane.

At the waiting private jet, the limo driver put her carry-on and briefcase on board the plane. Claire stood with a light wind whipping her skirt around her legs as she turned to Nick, who had just introduced her to the pilot and a flight attendant. As the two men walked toward the plane and left her with Nick, she turned to him. "I'll see you Friday night in Houston about half-past six."

Nick nodded. "I can't wait. Claire, I know that any anger and hard feelings will pass. I'm thrilled beyond anything I can possibly say to you."

"I'm glad, Nick. I think you'll love Cody the moment you meet him."

They gazed into each other's eyes and he was suddenly swamped with gratitude that she had given him a son. On impulse, he stepped closer to wrap his arms around her and kiss her.

He caught her by surprise, but then she slipped her arms around him and returned his kiss, a kiss that made him remember old times with her, that made him want to be with her longer and take the kiss deeper. His reaction was even stronger than it had been to their earlier kiss. Because of Claire, his life was suddenly filled with uncertainties and one of the biggest ones was how he was going to deal with her. For just a moment, he forgot the past, the present, the problems they'd have in the future. He wanted her.

Hot with desire, he tightened his arm around her slender waist as he parted her lips and his tongue mated with hers. Running his hand down her back and over her bottom, he wanted nothing more than to peel away the barriers of clothing between them. His heart pounded in his chest, so hard he thought it would burst. He trailed kisses to her throat as she leaned back to give him access to the slender column of her neck.

From somewhere deep in his mind came the warning to stop. If he didn't, he knew he'd take her right there on the tarmac.

Reluctantly he released her. He didn't want to fall in love again because he would be hurt all over again. Perhaps a deeper hurt this time. The problems between them now were bigger than ever. Not only was she still tethered to Houston and her family, they had a bigger issue to deal with. Their son. Nick told himself he couldn't get entangled again. As much as she tempted him, he had to resist kissing her when they were together. She was a huge threat to his happiness and his future in too many ways.

On a cerebral level he knew that. All too well. But on a physical level…how was he going to cope with this intense attraction he had to her?

Four

While her heart pounded, Claire looked into his blue eyes that had darkened with passion. She felt it in his hard body pressed close to hers, in his tongue that tangled with hers, in the arms that held her tight. And she responded in kind. Desire surged through her and stirred old memories she didn't want coming alive. Memories of making love to Nick long into the night, of waking in his arms the next day, only to repeat their heart-pounding performance. She tried to shut her mind to those remembrances, to his kisses, so that she could cool down and get her thoughts back where they needed to be. Back to thinking about the coming weekend.

It was going to be one of the most important weekends of her life. And certainly her son's life.

When she stepped back and under the lights on the tarmac, she could see his face clearly. On the ride over she'd given it some thought and now she wanted to tell him her plan. "Nick," she started, "you're welcome to stay with us.

I've got plenty of room in the house. I think it'd be best for Cody to get to know you with us around."

"Thanks," Nick said. "That sounds ideal, Claire. I'll take you up on that offer because staying there would let him get more accustomed to me in surroundings that are familiar to him."

"Actually, Nick, if all goes well, you might as well stay Saturday night, also. We can see how it goes on Friday. If I don't think you should stay, I'll tell you."

He smiled. "Fair enough. You know your son."

"Our son," she corrected, but she couldn't smile. She was hurt and she was frightened because Nick had had a bigger reaction than she had anticipated.

Glancing at the plane, she looked up at Nick. "I better board. They seem to be waiting."

"They are," he said, giving her a heavy-lidded look that stirred desire again. She stepped back, knowing she needed to avoid another kiss that would make her want things she couldn't have. Nick's kisses could always melt her. She had to keep a barrier around her heart because he was a heartbreaker.

"I'll see you Friday night. C'mon. I'll walk with you." He took her arm and they walked to the foot of the steps to the plane.

"See you, Nick," she said as she boarded. Taking a seat by a window she looked out at him and watched him as the plane taxied away. He stood there, the wind blowing locks of his dark brown hair. Hair so like Cody's. Maybe it was seeing that resemblance, maybe it was everything she'd been through this night. But the reality hit her hard, knocking her back into her seat. Cody really had a dad—a dad who wanted to know him.

What kind of dad would he be? What kind of rapport would he have with Cody? Questions bombarded her, not only about his relationship with Cody but with her. What would their future hold? Was he going to push for marriage, a paper marriage to satisfy the public so he could win his political race and become a United States Senator?

His political ambitions were daunting. Nick wanted to run for President of the United States. His dad had pushed for it and laid the groundwork years earlier. Nick and his father, the judge, embodied power, clout, wealth and success, and had built a network of cronies of the same type. Nick had stayed with the prestigious DC law firm just long enough to make lasting ties with some powerful people and then he had returned to his roots in Texas to build a strong support base.

She had known him long enough to know how he made friends with influential people who could help him. Some of Nick's socializing seemed to come as naturally to him as smiling. At the same time, there was the part of him that loved his ranch and cowboy life, who could soak that up as if it was necessary to restart his engines. Nick had always claimed ranching as his first love. What would he have done if his family, particularly his dad, hadn't pushed so hard for law and politics? If left to his own decisions as he had grown up, would Nick now be a rancher? She wondered how much of his current life was due to pleasing his family instead of doing what he wanted.

She recalled that he'd seemed the happiest when she had gone home with him to his ranch. He claimed he loved living and working on his ranch the most, but that wasn't what dominated his life now. But Nick wasn't the only one with contradictory aspects to his personality. She had them too. On the one hand she didn't want to think about Nick's kisses that still set her ablaze. She didn't want a marriage of convenience that made the most sense for Nick and would aid his political pursuits. One in which love would not be part of the union.

Yet, on the other hand, she couldn't let herself fall in love with Nick, or him with her. She knew that would only end up one way. With heartbreak. And she'd already lived through that agony once.

Life was truly complicated and had just gotten more so.

Because they had a child.

Nick was moving up politically, while she had a big business to run and her son and grandparents to care for. Whatever they did, she did not want to fall in love with Nick again. There had been no other man in her life because she had been busy with Cody, her family and running the business. Nick's kisses set her on fire and it was exciting to be with him, to have his arms around her, but that was lust, purely physical. It was not love. She'd remind herself of that time and time again, until she remembered it.

Sighing, she laid her head back on the seat as the plane reached cruising altitude. While she was grateful for the private flight that would get her home earlier, there was a part of her that actually dreaded going home. She'd have to break the news to her grandmother and then tell Cody. Cody would be happy, but her grandmother… Claire could almost script that conversation, and it wouldn't be good.

When she entered her house, she tiptoed into Cody's room and stood beside his bed. She wanted to hold him, to get him as close to her heart as possible. Tears threatened when she thought about having to share him with Nick now. She pulled a light blanket higher over him carefully while love for him enveloped her.

She didn't know how long she stood beside his bed watching him sleep. Finally, she went to her suite to shower and dress for the day.

By the time her gray-haired grandmother, Verna Prentiss, walked into the kitchen, Claire had made oatmeal, washed and sliced berries, and had everything set and ready. She gave her grandmother a light hug and kiss.

"I'm glad you're home and I'm glad it went well," Verna said. "Can you take today off, or even the morning before you go to the office?"

"I need to get to the office. I'll take off early this afternoon."

"Good. I'm glad. I'll see your grandfather today and take Cody with me. I'll tell him you'll see him tomorrow."

"Mom!" Cody exclaimed as he ran into the kitchen to hug her. She caught him, holding him lightly. Thin and wiry, he was still in pajamas. She kissed his cheek and then reluctantly let him go, fighting for control of her emotions.

As they ate breakfast, she listened to Cody tell her about building a spaceship out of boxes his great-grandmother had given him. As Cody and Verna talked, part of Claire's thoughts were on Nick and how he would see Cody. She was certain Nick would love his son wholeheartedly and want to be with him as much as possible.

After breakfast she said she would clear, but Verna shook her head. "I know you want to spend some time with Cody. Go ahead. This will give me something to do."

Laughing, Claire turned to Cody who was waiting and smiling. "Thanks," Claire said, and left with Cody who took her hand to show her his spaceship.

She sat on the floor playing with him, praising his spaceship. It was patched and pasted, but she knew he thought it was grand.

It was after nine when she told him she had to go to the office.

Brushing his brown hair off his forehead, she smiled at

him. "I'll take this afternoon off and we'll do something fun together. How's that?"

"Good," he said. "Can we take my spaceship outside and paint it?"

"That's a good idea. Let's go look in the garage and see what colors we have. If we don't have any paint, I'll get some while I'm out."

By the time she stood at the front door with Verna and Cody to tell them goodbye, it was approaching ten in the morning. "Kiss me goodbye." When he kissed her cheek, she wrapped her arms around him. Cody stepped back and his great-grandmother placed her hand on his shoulder.

"We'll see you this afternoon," her grandmother said, following her to the door to hold it open and wave goodbye as Claire hurried to her car. Before the front door closed, she had one last glimpse of Cody turning to run out of sight. Love for him swamped her again and she wished yesterday had never happened.

That night she read Cody his favorite bedtime story. Sitting beside him on his twin bed, which he'd dubbed his "big boy bed," she cuddled him close as she read about the caterpillar that ate a hole in everything. Her son giggled as he turned the pages, eager for what he knew was coming. He loved bugs and she'd read him this story about a hundred times. Each time was like the first time he heard it.

She cherished this time together. All day at work she looked forward to the hours they got to spend together each night. As she looked down at him now in the dim light, there was a part of her that wished she could keep him from Nick, that she could keep him to herself. But that was impossible. Now that Nick knew about his son, there was no going back.

But first she had to tell her grandmother about Nick.

She'd hold off on telling Cody until nearer to the time for Nick's visit because Cody would be too excited to wait. When she finally kissed him good-night and tiptoed from the room, she returned to the family room to rejoin her grandmother.

"Grandma, I want to tell you about the closing."

Pushing her bifocals higher on her nose, Verna looked up from her sewing. "Did everything go as you hoped?"

"Yes, except for one surprise," Claire replied, dreading breaking the news because it would forever change their lives, but putting off talking about it wouldn't change anything. "Grandma, the buyer's attorney was Nick Milan."

"Oh, my word," Verna said, putting down her needle. "I'm sure that was a surprise. Does he have children now?"

"No, he doesn't. His pregnant wife was killed two years ago in a car crash."

"Oh, no," Verna said, shaking her head. "He lost his wife and unborn baby? He's single and doesn't have any family?" Her empathy shone in her eyes.

"That's right." Claire took a deep breath and let the words flow. "Grandma, I had to tell him about Cody."

"Claire," she said, looking stricken. Tears filled her eyes and though she didn't say anything for a moment, Claire could feel her grandmother's concern wrap around her. Finally she gathered herself and added, "I'm sure he'll be here soon to meet Cody."

"That's right. He's flying in Friday to meet his son and take us out to dinner. You're invited for dinner too. He'll be here for the weekend and leave Sunday."

"No, that should be just you and Cody. I'll call my sister. Becky will pick me up." She paused a moment, emotion choking off her words. "Claire, I—"

She could see the tears in her grandmother's eyes and knew exactly how she felt. She was worried for Claire, worried how things would fall once Nick met his son. Claire felt it, too. But she needed to reassure her grandmother, not bask in her self-pity. "We'll work things out, so please don't worry about it. Nick is a nice person."

"I'll try not to, but I can't keep from worrying and I know you're worried. Go ahead and tell Grandpa tomorrow when you see him. It'll give him something to think about and pray over."

"I'll tell him if the opportunity arises. If he's with his cronies, I'll do it another day."

Her grandmother nodded. "I suppose Nick was terribly shocked. I know you felt you had to tell him. Was he angry you hadn't told him earlier?"

"Yes, he was at first, but it didn't last," Claire answered.

"He may want Cody the majority of the time."

"I don't think that will happen. We'll just work out a way to share Cody. I think Nick will be a good dad."

Her grandmother started crying and Claire, hurting for her, crossed the room to hug her. "Don't cry. We don't know how much we'll see of Nick and he has clearly said he will not take Cody from me."

"We can't fight the Milans. They're powerful people."

"We won't have to," Claire said, hoping her words proved true. "Please don't cry," Claire repeated, taking her grandmother in her arms again and noticing how much more frail and thin she was.

Her grandmother wiped her eyes as she sat back. "I'm all right and don't you worry. We'll just take each day as it comes. I'll pray for the best."

Claire nodded. "We all will. I wanted to tell you before I tell Cody. I expect him to be very happy about the news because he'll never think of the downside to this. I know he'll be eager and excited," she said, hoping that's what Cody would feel.

* * *

Claire took the day off Friday. Her grandmother had already gone for the weekend. During the afternoon Claire sat with Cody on her lap.

"Cody, I want to tell you something." His big blue eyes looked up at her and she smiled, hugging him lightly. He wore a superhero T-shirt, jeans and his tennis shoes, and she knew he wanted to run and play. "I saw your daddy this weekend. Here is a picture of me with him. His name is Nicholas Milan."

"He's my daddy?"

"Yes. And he is coming to see you tonight."

"This is my daddy and he's coming here?" Cody asked, grinning, his eyes sparkling and looking as if he had just been given a trip to Disneyland. From that moment on until it was time for Nick's arrival, Cody was giddy with excitement.

She gave Cody new Legos and left him building while she got dressed, thinking that one plus to Cody's exhilaration was she didn't have time to grow steadily more nervous about seeing Nick.

Finally, she made one last check of herself, her gaze roaming over her black hair, which fell to her shoulders. She wore a dark red cotton dress with a V neckline, a straight skirt that ended at her knees and matching high-heeled shoes. In spite of butterflies in her stomach, icy hands and a sense of dread, she felt a streak of excitement to see Nick again. An excitement she tried to ignore.

When the bell rang, she hurried to open the door, aware of Cody following her instructions and waiting in the family room. Her heartbeat spiked as she looked into Nick's blue eyes. His smile quickened her breathing. In his navy suit and matching tie, he was handsome. Too handsome, too irresistible. Taking another deep breath, she opened the storm door. "Come in, Nick. Cody is excited and there's no calming him."

"I'm excited, too," Nick said, his gaze sweeping over her. "You look beautiful, Claire," he said, his voice taking on a husky note. He glanced over her head. "Where's your grandmother?"

"She thought we should be alone for this momentous occasion, so she's gone to her sister's house for the weekend."

"That was perceptive of her," he said. "It will be good to have just the three of us. I'll thank her for understanding."

Claire glanced beyond him and noticed a white limo parked on the drive. "You came in a limo? Is the driver just going to sit in the car and wait until we go to dinner? I can drive to dinner and you can send him on his way now."

"I made arrangements for the limo through dinner and afterward, when we get back here, I'll send him away for the night. He's leaving now and I'll call him to come get us when we're ready to go. I thought Cody might like a limo ride. Has he ever ridden in one?"

"No, he hasn't and he will probably love it. He's curious."

Nick set his things down inside the door. "I brought champagne for us later, to celebrate," he said, handing her an insulated box. She was aware of the brush of his warm fingers as she took the box.

"I have presents for Cody, too, but I'd like to leave those until after I've met him."

"You might as well, because right now he is more curious about you and he won't pay attention to presents until he's met you. I told him to wait in the family room and I'd bring you in." She glanced toward the room where Cody awaited. "Let's go meet your son," she said.

She linked her arm in Nick's to take him inside, knowing that her life, as well as Nick's, was about to change forever.

Five

Nick couldn't recall a time he had felt so unprepared to meet someone, even though he wanted this more than anything else in life. He would love Cody on sight, but he didn't know how to deal with meeting his son.

Since telling Claire goodbye, he had spent the past couple of days getting ready for this moment. They entered the family room and all Nick's qualms melted away as he looked at a small boy who bore enough Milan family resemblance that there could never be a doubt about his heritage. Cody's blue eyes were large and he smiled as he watched Nick approach.

"Cody, come here," Claire said in a sweet voice. The boy ran to her. Setting the box with the champagne on a table, she placed her hand on his shoulder. "I want to introduce you to somebody," she said, "and then I'll just go into the kitchen for a few minutes. Okay?"

He looked up at her. "Yes, ma'am," he said, his curious gaze returning to Nick.

"Cody, this is your dad, Nick Milan. Nick, here's your son, Cody," she said. Then she stepped away and Nick didn't see her pick up the champagne and leave because his attention was on the small boy staring at him.

With a lump in his throat, Nick smiled and walked to Cody. He hunkered down in front of him to get closer to Cody's level. "You're my son, Cody, and I love you," Nick said in a husky voice.

"Yes, sir," Cody said quietly.

Nick's insides clutched. "Cody, can I hug you?" he asked, thinking that was the first time in his life he could recall asking permission for a hug.

Cody nodded. "Yes, sir."

With a pounding heart filled with joy and trepidation, Nick hugged him lightly. "You're my son, Cody," Nick repeated. "You'll never know how wonderful that is for me." He released the little boy. "You can think about what you want to call me—Dad or Daddy. I hope one of those will be what you'd like best. What do you think?"

Cody stared at him a few minutes that made Nick tense. What if Cody didn't want to call him either? He waited, feeling as if he couldn't catch his breath.

"Dad," he said with a nod of his head. "Okay?"

"It's more than okay. It's great. I can't tell you how wonderful it will be to hear you call me that. It means you're my little boy. Let's find your mom and get her to join us. She doesn't need to stay away. You want to go get her?"

"Yes, sir," Cody replied, nodding and running out of the room.

As Nick watched Cody go, he was overwhelmed by emotion. He'd loved Cody the first moment he saw him. He felt he couldn't get enough of seeing or being with him. Now that he knew of his existence, he wanted to be with Cody every day.

He thought about what Claire had said the other day, how his father would push for a marriage of convenience. Claire had been cool on the subject, and Nick hadn't given it much thought, but now he realized it would solve a lot of problems. Though, he had to admit, far more for him than for her. All the same problems faced them, plus more. If they married and it didn't work out, a split would mean a divorce and even more bitterness than their previous breakup. If they had a marriage of convenience, could he keep from falling in love with her and getting hurt all over again? No, he couldn't see a marriage of convenience working, or Claire ever agreeing.

Nick walked to the front entry to pick up an armload of wrapped presents and returned to the family room. He had been so taken with Cody, he hadn't really looked at the tall Christmas tree in a corner of the room. Decorations included a lot of children's ornaments and a paper chain probably made by Cody. There were already presents scattered around the base. Usually Christmas was a painful, lonely time for Nick, but he looked forward to it this year, with Cody in it. That is, if he could work it out with Claire.

In minutes Cody appeared, holding Claire's hand. "Cody said you sent him to tell me to join you."

"You might as well. Getting to know each other will take time. Cody, I brought you some presents. They're all in this sack. You can get them out and open them now."

"Nick, let's have a seat while we watch him open his presents," Claire said, sitting and crossing the long legs that he couldn't keep from noticing. She had the best legs of any woman he had ever known.

Cody sent him a questioning look and then turned to Claire, who nodded. "Go ahead and open your presents."

The first one was a book that Cody opened carefully,

but when he saw what it was, he smiled and held it up for Claire to see. "Mama, look at this."

"One of your favorites that you've been wanting," she said, smiling at Nick who was relieved that the first gift had been something Cody really wanted. Claire had sent him a list, but he still had felt uncertain.

Cody turned to him. "Thank you."

"You're welcome, Cody."

Cody set aside the book and pulled another bigger package out of the sack and tore it open to show Claire a box of Legos. "I don't have this one. Thank you," he said to Nick, smiling at him and looking at the box. "Can I do this now, Mama?"

"Open all your presents and then you may play with whatever you want," Claire said. "Let's see what else you have in the sack."

With each gift Cody ripped the paper away faster and with more enthusiasm. He pulled out one that had a stuffed monkey on a spring that he could send flying across the room. He put it on the spring and pulled the lever and the monkey shot into the air, startling Claire and sending the boy into peals of laughter.

"Cody," Claire said. "Not in the house."

"Yeah," Nick agreed. "Maybe we should try that one in the backyard, Cody."

"Yes, sir," Cody said, giggling and getting another present.

"Is this more of the same?" Claire asked, eyeing the odd shape of the next gift.

"Close, but it stays on the floor," Nick replied, looking at Cody laugh with his blue eyes sparkling and thinking he had the most adorable son possible. Cody pulled a long furry toy with black eyes and a smiling mouth. When he pushed the switch the fuzzy toy rolled around on the floor while it growled, which made Cody laugh out loud. He flopped down on the floor beside it to watch.

Charmed by Cody, Nick glanced at Claire and she looked back while she laughed and shook her head. For an instant he felt a bond with her. They had a son, and for the moment they seemed like a family. Gratitude to Claire filled him. Nick had felt grateful to her before, but it was magnified a thousandfold now that he was with both of them.

Cody opened another present. "Mama, look," he cried, jumping up to take a box to her.

"A child's computer just for you, Cody. You'll have such fun with that," she said, smiling at him as he tried to open the box. While she peeled away tape, he turned to Nick.

"Thank you for my present," he said, smiling at Nick. Cody pulled out the last box and ripped away paper to hold up a bug collecting kit that included a net.

"Super," he said. "Look, I can catch some bugs," he said, taking the kit to Claire.

"You did well, Nick. These are all perfect little-boy gifts. And he loves them all."

"Thanks. I had help from a long-time friend who has a three-year-old son." He'd have to remember to thank his close friend Mike Calhoun for the suggestions the next time he saw him.

"Looks like you asked an expert," she said, smiling at him.

"Can we build this now?" Cody asked, pulling the Lego box out from beneath his other presents and holding it out to Nick.

"Claire, what's the schedule? Can we start on this?"

"We'll go to dinner whenever you two are ready. I'm in no hurry."

Nick turned to the boy. "Okay, Cody, let's give it thirty

minutes and then I'll take you and your mother to dinner. How's that?"

"Super," Cody said, starting out of the room.

"I guess I'm supposed to follow," Nick said to Claire, who nodded.

"He's headed to the kitchen table. He's used to playing with his grandmother. She doesn't sit on the floor."

"Come join us."

"Oh, no, this is male bonding time," she said. When he didn't move right away she added, "If you don't get in there, he'll be through."

Nick stood up to leave, but stopped. "Claire, he's wonderful. He has to be the cutest kid on the whole Earth."

"Thanks. I think so too. And I can tell he's very happy to have a dad," she said. Despite her fleeting smile, she looked as if there was something worrying her and he wondered if she was unhappy that Cody knew about him. On the other hand, Nick was so overwhelmed with gratitude he wanted to cross the room, hug and reassure her so she wouldn't worry. But she had thrown up a wall between them, which was what he should also do. They were both in a vulnerable state right now and they had to be careful. With Claire, a simple kiss might lead to falling in love. And that could end in more hurt.

He left her, and when he joined his son in the kitchen, even though she had warned him, it startled him how much Cody had done by himself. He'd followed the diagrams and was working away with success.

As Nick pulled a chair beside him, Cody tossed him a smile and returned to fitting the next block into place.

Nick helped, talking with Cody, finding him easy to be with and as happy as Claire had indicated. She had done a great job raising him. What an incredible woman she was, a woman who—

He pulled the plug on that thought as he felt his heart skip a beat. He couldn't keep thinking about her as a desirable woman, wanting to touch her, to kiss her. He had to listen to common sense. It warned him to avoid falling in love again because it would be futile, another giant heartbreak he had to avoid.

After almost half an hour, Cody showed Nick his room and other creations he had built. Claire appeared, standing in the doorway. "I hate to interrupt, but before you know it, bedtime will come for Cody. We should go to dinner unless you'd like to eat here."

"No," Nick answered. "Cody, let's go to dinner. We'll look at this later or next time," he said.

"Yes, sir," Cody said as Nick's phone buzzed. He pulled it from his pocket to look at it and walked away from them to take a business call.

"You wash your hands before we go," Claire said to Cody, and he ran out of the room. Nick finished his call, returning to join Claire in the family room. She stood at the window with her back to him and his gaze ran over her again, causing desire to flare. He couldn't stop his response to her any more than he could stop breathing. She heard him and turned, her dark eyes riveting, making him draw a deep breath. He had to fight the urge to take her into his arms, stopping himself within a few feet of her.

"He's the happiest kid ever. You've done a wonderful job, Claire," Nick said, feeling another rush of gratitude to her for having Cody, for raising him to be such a polite, happy little boy, for telling him about Cody. It frightened Nick to think that she could have gone home without telling him and he might not have known about his son for years longer, if ever.

"Thank you, but I don't think I can take credit for his

disposition. I think he may have inherited it." She winked at him. "But who knows?"

When Cody returned, they donned their coats, and as they walked to the front door, Nick picked up Cody, carrying him easily. "Have you ever ridden in a limousine?"

"No, sir," he said, his eyes widening as he glanced toward the front door.

"Well, you're going to now."

Cody turned quickly to grin at Claire who had to laugh. "I think that grin means he's enthused."

"Good. Let's go see," Nick said, opening the front door and swinging Cody down to stand him on his feet.

"Wow," Cody said, standing stock-still and staring agape at the limo.

Nick was delighted with Cody's reaction and they took time, before they left Claire's house, for Cody to look at everything in the interior of the limo. Nick showed him the phone and the bar, the sliding glass divider, and all the hidden gadgets. He introduced the chauffeur and finally they buckled up and left.

From that moment until they reached the restaurant, Cody didn't say a word. He spent the whole time looking intently at everything Nick had shown him, causing Nick to chuckle. "I'm not sure he knows we're riding with him," he told Claire. "I had no idea this would be so fascinating to him."

"My guess is you've been in limos so much of your life, you don't remember the first time you rode in one."

"You're right and if it was with my dad, I wasn't investigating everything in sight. I promise you that."

As they smiled at each other, he recalled old times with her when they had shared so much laughter. Nick remembered when he had taken her to the family ranch after his parents had moved to Dallas. He and Claire had gone horseback riding at sunrise and the morning had been one of his happiest memories. They had ridden to one of his favorite places, where he had gone as a boy when he wanted to be alone. When they rode into the small clearing near the creek, a skunk had been stretched on a boulder, enjoying the morning. Nick had laughed with Claire as they rode away and left the skunk to enjoy the hideaway.

As the limo slowed to a stop at the restaurant and the valet opened their door, Nick's attention returned to the present.

They entered the restaurant that had a jungle ambience, thunder rumbling and lightning flashing, the staged animals roaring. Cody seemed lost in his own world through dinner.

As soon as they finished, they returned to the limo, and an overexcited Cody snuggled up to Claire and in minutes he crashed, falling into a deep sleep.

When the limo wound up her drive, Nick took a moment to look at the large home that he hadn't really noticed when he'd arrived earlier. The rambling two-story house was set back on a perfectly landscaped lawn with tall trees that now twinkled with Christmas lights. "You have a beautiful home, Claire. You've done well."

"Thanks. I've had a lot of luck in business, I guess. I started as a kid helping at Grandpa's office so when I finished college and came into the business, I had all sorts of wonderful contacts through him."

"You had to do a lot yourself. Wonderful contacts from your grandfather are a fine background, but you've gone way beyond what success he had."

"Fortunately, people who've been happy working with me tell their friends, so my network builds. I love my work and in spite of a 24/7 business, I get a lot of hours with Cody."

"That's good," Nick said.

When the limo stopped, Claire looked down at her sleeping son. "It's past his bedtime and he has been so excited all day. Give me a minute to wake him and he'll walk in."

"No. He's a featherweight. I'll carry him." Nick picked him up easily, and in his sleep Cody wrapped his arm around Nick's neck.

Nick paused to make arrangements with the driver to come back Saturday night in time to take them to dinner. Then he entered the front door Claire held open and carried Cody up to his room and placed him on the bed.

Claire stepped forward to get him ready for bed. "Want some help?" he asked her.

She shook her head. "No, but thanks. I'll just get his shoes and socks off and leave him alone. I'm sure he's worn out."

Nick stepped away, strolling around Cody's room, looking at shelves of family pictures of the boy with his great-grandparents, with his grandmother and with Claire. Through one doorway Nick could see an attached bathroom, but he went through the other door into an adjoining playroom filled with toys, bookshelves and a large fish tank that seemed to take center stage. Cody had a large rocking horse, plastic superheroes on the shelves and a life-size mural of Winnie-the-Pooh characters on one wall.

A door was open to an adjoining bedroom and he realized it was Claire's suite. She had a four-poster bed with a canopy, and as his gaze ran over the bed and mound of pillows, he could picture her sprawled there. He remembered how she had looked in bed, recalling her black hair spread over the pillow beside him. His insides tightened as the memories ignited desire.

Nick turned to look at her as she leaned over Cody and his gaze ran down her backside, the straight skirt of her dress fitting her hips snugly and the long legs that peeked from under her dress as she leaned over. He could feel his body heat up as he looked at her. She could still cause a reaction in him on a physical level, something no other women he had dated had done since his loss of Karen. And he'd bet Claire still had a physical response to him, too.

Logically, he could enumerate each and every reason to avoid her, but nothing could stop his body from responding to her, from desiring her. She was a sexy, beautiful woman who took his breath away. He turned abruptly, knowing he had to get her out of his thoughts. That wouldn't happen as long as he stood there staring at her long legs and remembering how they felt wrapped around his waist as they made love.

When he looked back, she had stepped away from Cody's bed. His gaze shifted to Cody, who was sleeping soundly, his dark hair falling over his forehead. Nick wanted his son in his life. He would try to cooperate with Claire, but he had to be part of Cody's life. He'd loved Cody from the first moment he saw him this afternoon.

Claire stepped toward him. "Let's go downstairs," she said softly.

When they walked into the hall, she touched his sleeve lightly to get his attention. "You can have the suite across the hall from us for the weekend," she said, stopping to switch on the lights in the room she pointed out. He poked his head in and saw a large living area done in deep blues with hardwood floors and area rugs.

"There's an adjoining bath and bedroom, giving you

your own suite," she explained. "Down the hall are two more bedroom suites and I have an office on this floor, too."

"Claire, this is a splendid house. Very luxurious, but comfortable and practical at the same time."

"I know a lot of builders, so I tried to get the best."

He smiled and ran his finger along her smooth cheek. "Good businesswoman."

"I try to be."

For whatever reason, seeing her there, backlit by the lamp in the suite, in her element in her own home that she'd built with her successful career, he was more drawn to her than ever. More than anything he wanted to lean down and kiss her. He stepped closer, unable to resist her allure, but before he could make his move, Claire stepped back. She was keeping a wall between them. She was polite, friendly, cooperative in a lot of ways about Cody, but Nick felt that, beneath the surface, she wished he would pack and go back to Dallas and get out of her life.

"Come on," she said. "Let's go downstairs. I have a monitor for Cody so I can hear if he wakes. I have an alarm that lets me know if he gets out of his bed and walks around his room. I also can see him on my iPad, so I know when he's sleeping peacefully."

"You've covered all your bases to keep him safe, I see." He followed her down the hall.

"You were very good with Cody," she said as they reached the ground floor.

"He's an easy, wonderful kid. I'm in awe, Claire. He's perfect. I know I've got a prejudiced view, but I can't think of one thing about him that isn't really great."

She laughed. "You sound just like a new dad. But you're right—he's easy, likeable and a smart little boy. And he's glad to have his dad in his life," she said. "You had the perfect gifts and the limo was the crowning touch."

"Mike suggested the limo."

"Mike sounds like a good dad. Would you like a drink?"

"It's time to break out the champagne so we can celebrate." His fingers closed on her arm to stop her and she turned to look up at him. His heart beat faster as he looked down at her. "I want you to celebrate, Claire. I don't want this to be an unhappy or difficult event to bring me into Cody's life. I know it means you have to share him, but I'll try every way I can to make that a plus for you and for Cody." Her brown eyes were wide and dark and mysterious. He couldn't read them. Nor could he keep from letting his gaze drift to her mouth that was enticing, bow-shaped with full lips that were so soft, yet fiery. He felt caught in her gaze and she must have felt the same because her eyes widened slightly and then her gaze lowered to his mouth and his heart pounded.

They were only a foot apart and it would be easy to close that gap and give into the temptation that clawed at him. So easy to touch his lips to hers and taste the sweetness that was Claire. If only…

No, he couldn't. He had to fight the temptation. It was for his own good. Reluctantly he stepped away. "Where's the champagne?" he asked, his voice far deeper and hoarse.

She gave him a searching look and finally spoke. "In the bar," she whispered, turning abruptly. "I'll get it." She went behind the bar in the far corner of the family room. He trailed behind her and stood in the entrance, watching her. She looked lost, as if she had never been in the place before, as she glanced around. Shaking her shoulders, she reached for a glass and her hand trembled.

Grasping her slender wrist lightly, Nick steadied her hand and reached beyond her to get two crystal flutes. He turned her to face him. He ached to kiss her and he fought an inner battle, wondering if her own inner battle was causing her to look upset and shaky.

"Go sit and I'll pour the champagne," he said, starting to open the bottle while trying to resist reaching for her. She nodded and stepped away, moving out of the bar to sit on a high stool.

He let out his breath. How was he going to keep from falling in love again? Usually he recalled their parting, the anger and hurt that always cooled his desire for her, but it wasn't working tonight. He set two empty flutes in front of her, popped the cork and poured the pale, bubbly champagne.

He walked around to face her, leaving a yard of space between them so he wouldn't be tempted. He raised his flute. "Here's to you, Claire, a beautiful woman."

She gave him a tight smile. "Thank you. That isn't what I thought you'd say."

He touched her flute with his. Watching her, he sipped his champagne. He wanted to set his flute down, take hers from her and pull her into his arms. That was the way to pain and he wasn't going to do it, but his inner battle was tearing him up.

"Here's to our son, a beautiful child."

"I'll drink to that one," she said, smiling broadly and looking as if she'd relaxed slightly.

"That's better."

Only one lamp was on in the large room, spilling a soft glow, and she had switched on classical music in the background.

"This next toast is to celebrate the night I met my son." He held out his glass again.

"Whatever happens, Nick, I know you'll be a good dad."

They tapped glasses and then he sipped the bubbly champagne. Too bad he couldn't cool his desire or his reactions to her as easily as the champagne quenched his thirst. She sat on the barstool, her fabulous legs crossed. He ought to stop looking, but she was too beautiful, too easy to look at.

Nick set aside his glass and crossed the room to the briefcase that he'd brought with him. He opened it and removed two small boxes.

He returned to hand her a long, flat box and place the smaller box on a table. "This is for you. I wasn't with you when you had Cody. I should have been, but we can't undo the past. I wish I could have given you this when he was born. It's a small token of gratitude."

"Nick, you didn't need to get me something," she said, shaking her head.

"Go ahead. It's your gift for being Cody's mother. Cody got his presents. Now I want you to have your gifts—what I would have given you if I had been present at his birth."

"That's sweet, Nick." She carefully untied the ribbon and paper, opening the box with a gasp. "Oh, Nick, this is beautiful," she said. He moved closer to take out the gold chain with a diamond heart pendant made with three heart-shaped rows of diamonds and a larger diamond in the center. The pendant glittered in the subdued light.

"Can I put it on you?"

"Of course," she said, smiling at him. "It's stunning."

"You're stunning, Claire," he said quietly. "More now than four years ago." As she lifted her hair out of his way, Nick stepped behind her to fasten the necklace.

She turned to face him. Her big, dark eyes held him and memories hit him with almost physical force as he recalled how much he had loved her once. "Claire, my heart has been broken twice—first with you and then when I lost my baby and my wife. I can't go through heartbreak again."

"We were both hurt," she whispered. "We can't undo the past. Don't try."

"I'm not trying to undo the past, Claire. And for this weekend, let's put aside trying to work out our future. Let's just get reacquainted and let me get to know my son. I want to make the most of each moment and not worry about how we'll move forward. Can we do that?"

"Of course. That sounds best to me." She gave him a slight smile. She fingered the diamond. "Can I go look in the mirror at my new necklace? It's beautiful. Thank you."

"You have another present. Go ahead and open it."

She carefully opened a smaller box to find a gold charm bracelet with a one-carat diamond imbedded in the gold between each charm. One charm was a baby in a small crib and inscribed on the crib were the tiny numbers of Cody's birthday. Another charm was a birthday cake with one candle followed by a charm in the shape of a small boy, then three figures, a man and a woman with a small boy between them. She smiled as she touched it. "That's special, Nick. Thank you."

"I'll add a charm each year until Nick is eighteen, but you can pick out what you want for the charms."

She turned the bracelet in her hand. "You're committing yourself for the coming years. You don't know what you'll be doing." She looked up at him. "Let's sit down," she said, moving to a chair. He sat close beside her, a table between them where they set their drinks.

"Nick, are there any grandchildren in the Milan family yet, besides Cody?"

"No. Cody is the first grandchild."

"Oh, my word," she said, rubbing her arms as if she were freezing. "Then for sure your father is going to push you to marry me. He won't want you to take no for an answer."

Nick frowned. "I'm sure you're right. You're out of his

reach, although he might contact you. My dad interfered a lot in my sister's life when she fell in love with her husband, Jake, but Dad's older now, more mellow, less energetic."

Sighing, Claire shook her head. "I don't want to deal with your father. I can if I have to, and I'm not going to marry you because your dad wants us to, but if Cody is the only grandchild and you're headed for a big political life, you know that's what's coming."

"I'm a grown man and I can make my own decisions."

"You've always pleased him. You told me that. You're very close."

"We are, but I have to live my life. I'm not going through hell to please my dad. I don't want another broken heart and I know you're deeply involved in your life, as I am in mine—even more than we were four years ago. Besides, I'll work out a way for them to see their grandson and they'll settle down eventually."

"I don't think so, Nick. There's more than seeing a grandson. There's your political career at stake."

"Stop worrying until it gets to be a problem," he said. "Right now, Dad doesn't know Cody exists."

She shook her head. "Why do I feel like I'm headed for disaster?"

"It'll be all right, Claire," he said to reassure her. But deep inside he wondered if they were, indeed, headed for disaster. She was right on target about his dad. Nick just had to head off his dad trying to contact her or, worse, bribe her, which would only anger Claire more and cause worse feelings.

He had to change the subject before she read his own fears on his face. "Now, tell me more about your life and Cody's."

"I think you mean, tell you more about Cody," she said,

smiling at him. She settled back to talk about an incident when Cody was a baby and from that on to other moments in his life. Nick listened intently, but he watched her, remembering, taken back to times before. They had seldom spent hours just talking like this because they kissed as much as possible, which always led to making love.

Something he shouldn't be thinking about, he chided himself. It conjured up steamy memories that made him want to pull her into his arms and kiss her until he could carry her to his bed. How could she still have this intense physical effect on him? Was it because he'd been without a woman in his life for the last two years? Or was it because it was Claire?

He reined in his errant thoughts and focused on formulating a full picture of his son's first three years of life as Claire regaled him with stories, some funny, some touching. Eventually, she stood.

"Nick, it's one o'clock in the morning and this day has been long and emotional. It's time to call it a night."

"Today has been nerve-racking for all adults concerned," he said, standing beside her. "Cody was the happy one, thank heavens. It worked out better than I hoped." They left the room and Claire switched off the light.

He gathered his carry-on and briefcase, turning to join her at the foot of the stairs.

"I'll switch on the alarm down here. Want anything before I do?"

"No. Not at all," he said, watching her punch buttons on her phone. When he started upstairs with her, it seemed natural to drape his free arm across her slender shoulders. The moment he touched her, he realized his mistake and pulled back.

At her door he set his things on the floor. As if he hadn't just chastised himself for touching her, he placed his hands on her shoulders. "Thanks again, Claire," he said, aware of her warm shoulders beneath her blouse. Her mouth was rosy, too tempting. It amazed him how much he wanted to kiss her and hold her close. He wanted to out of gratitude, and even more, he wanted to because she was an appealing, gorgeous, sexy woman and he could remember how her kisses had pleasured him.

"Nick, thank you for the necklace," she said, touching it briefly. "It's beautiful."

He looked at the necklace, knowing what it represented and knowing he would have showered her with more if he had been present at the time of Cody's birth. He had to stop looking back, but it was difficult when he had learned about Cody only days earlier.

"He's absolutely wonderful. Think about taking a week off and bringing him to Dallas so we can get to know each other better. We can stay several days on the ranch if you think he'd like that."

"He'd love it," Claire said. "What little boy wouldn't love it on a ranch? Especially with you doting on him."

"Then think about spending the whole time there. He'll have a wonderful time and I know you used to like being on the ranch."

"I did," she answered.

"So do I. Now more than ever."

"You were a success tonight, Nick. I think he's going to love having you for a dad."

He smiled. "We did all right tonight, didn't we?"

She returned his grin briefly, but the worry didn't leave her expression. "I suppose we did. The tough decisions are still ahead, though."

He nodded and she tilted her head toward her door. "Nick, it's late." When he stepped back, she said, "I'm an early riser. You can go downstairs and the coffee will be brewed by six. Is that early enough because I can go down an hour sooner if you'd like?"

"Six is perfect. Thank you for tonight. You did all you could to make this easy for me." Nick brushed a kiss on her forehead and looked into her eyes. Moments like this reminded him of what he'd missed, but he was doing better at putting the past behind him. "The more time I have with Cody, the sooner I'll stop longing for what might have been. Tomorrow I'll invite him to the ranch."

She nodded. "Good night, Nick," she said and stepped into her room.

He picked up his things and crossed the hall, shutting himself into his suite and letting out his breath. He couldn't spend a lot of time around her. Each time with her he had to fight the temptation to kiss her. And it was getting more and more difficult.

"Dammit," he whispered, finally giving vent to feelings that had threatened him during the evening. Claire had him tied in knots. He would take them to his ranch, which stirred memories of the week he had taken Claire to the family ranch when they had been so wildly in love. He thought about the hours they had made love there and he ached, wanting her and wondering how he was going to keep from being hurt worse than ever.

Nick raked his fingers through his hair. What did she feel? Right now, was she locked in as much turmoil over him as he was over her?

As worry filled her, Claire covered her face with her hands. Nick was appealing, sexy and he was being good to her. How was she going to avoid falling deeply in love again? And hurt even worse than before?

She was still attracted physically to Nick. Every touch had been sizzling; the light, impersonal kisses that were so meaningless to Nick had made her breathless. She didn't want to respond to him, didn't want to have her life tied in with his constantly. She couldn't forget his political ambitions. Cody's birth so close to Nick's marriage would hurt him in politics, and he'd need to marry her to smooth things over for the political races he faced. He said politics didn't matter, but she didn't believe him. Whatever Nick felt, his father was going to push Nick to marry her.

Nick wanted her to take a week and go to Dallas, to his ranch. Could she cope with being under the same roof with Nick for a week? She stood in the middle of her room, staring into space, remembering being on the ranch with Nick and how in love they had been. Memories would be intense and make it even more difficult to resist him.

Finally she began to get ready for bed, barely thinking about what she was doing because her thoughts were on Nick and how to deal with him. She turned back her bed and returned to the sitting room to switch off the light. Before she did, she saw the glitter of the heart-shaped pendant on her dresser and she crossed the room to pick it up. It had cost Nick a lot, she thought as she looked at the sparkling diamonds catching the light. Turning off the light, she carried the necklace and placed it on her night table before she got into bed. Nick was too appealing in too many ways. She couldn't see how she could avoid loving him…and that was the problem.

Six

Claire had coffee brewing when Nick walked through the kitchen door the next morning. In jeans, boots and a plaid, cotton shirt, he looked more approachable and still as handsome as ever. "You don't wear jeans often."

He crossed the kitchen to her. "I don't recall seeing you in jeans a lot of times, either. I have to say, they look infinitely better on you."

"I beg to differ, but thanks," she said, smiling at him, glad to see him relaxed and more at ease than yesterday.

"I have tickets reserved for all of us at the aquarium. If you don't think Cody would like that, I'll cancel and we'll do something else."

"Cody will love it. I've meant to take him, but just haven't done it. He's sleeping late. I guess he was worn out last night."

"So how did his mama sleep?" Nick asked, getting himself a cup of coffee and standing close.

"Fair. There's no way to turn off worries," she said quietly.

Setting down his coffee mug, he placed his hands on the counter on either side of her, hemming her in so he had her full attention. As her heartbeat accelerated, he leaned down to look directly into her eyes.

"Let's get back to the cheerful morning. You and I can be friends. We were once. There's no rush here. I can take my time getting to know Cody. I'm not pushing you and I have no deadlines where Cody is concerned. As much as we can, let's put the past behind us," he said, giving her a crooked smile.

"I'll try." Inside she was hurting more than ever, because he was so understanding, which only made him more appealing. She felt on track for a giant wreck to her heart. He stood too close, only inches away. She couldn't keep from looking at his mouth, thinking about his kisses. She drew a deep breath and looked up to find him watching her with desire blatant in his expression.

"This is life altering and I'm trying to get accustomed to the change of having you in our lives," she said, looking into his sexy, thickly lashed blue eyes, which had always captivated her. Why was she so susceptible to Nick? Her heart started racing the moment he stepped into the room and sped up again when he moved close.

"Okay, but keep in mind, I'm not pushing. We don't have to rush to make changes."

"Thank you for that concession." She could barely get out the words, yet she didn't want to ask him to move away and make more of an issue of her reaction to him.

He wrapped his arms around her lightly. "We'll work something out we can both live with."

She didn't answer. It was easy to say they would work things out, but it was going to be difficult to actually do it. Nick had hurt her badly years ago and she couldn't bear another big heartbreak. "I should get breakfast, Nick."

She moved away to stir the oatmeal she'd put on the stove.

Nick still held the appeal he once had and there was no way to stop her reactions to him. Each response would be a deeper hurt when they couldn't work out being together. She still couldn't leave Houston and Nick wouldn't leave Dallas, Washington, DC, or Austin now or in years to come if he was elected—and he would be. With a child between them life would be more complicated than ever. Not only could she be hurt, so could Cody.

Cody skipped into the room with his stuffed tiger beneath one arm. He wore his pajamas and had the bug net Nick had given him in his other hand.

"Good morning," Claire said, hugging him and wanting to keep holding him, but she let him go. He turned to look at Nick who picked him up.

"I have tickets to the aquarium today. How does that sound?"

Cody looked expectantly at Claire. "It's where they have big tanks," she explained. "Way bigger than the one you have and they hold fish bigger than you."

He turned to grin at Nick. "I'd like that. I have little fish."

"I saw your fish, and after breakfast you can show me your fish tank and tell me about your fish. Do you know what kind you have?"

"Yes, sir, I do," Cody said.

Nick set him on his feet and Cody put the net and his tiger on one chair as he climbed into his booster seat. Then Nick pushed him under the table. "I'm going to need to get one of these chairs at my house. Probably at the ranch, too."

Startled, she glanced at the booster seat. She hadn't

thought about Nick having to get equipment and toys for Cody, but she supposed he would if he planned to have him part of the time. For an instant it made the change seem more real and imminent. Nick glanced at her and she turned away quickly, but in seconds, he was beside her, taking the spoon from her hand. "I'll stir the oatmeal now. You play with Cody or do whatever you would like to do."

"Thanks, Nick," she said, certain he had guessed she was upset.

As Nick helped her get breakfast, he turned to her. "I called the limo driver I have for the weekend and he'll take us to the aquarium today."

"We're going in the limo?" she asked, and before Nick could answer, Cody asked the same question.

He looked so hopeful she had to smile as Nick nodded. "Yes, we are, Cody."

Cody beamed with pleasure while she shook her head. "Next week may be very dull around here."

"Then make arrangements and come to Dallas next week. You own the company, so get someone else to run it."

"You know it isn't that easy when I have appointments, closings and things to do. I'll check my calendar after breakfast."

"Give me the word and I'll arrange my schedule so I can be off and we can go to the ranch. Cody, would you like to spend a few days on my ranch?"

"Yes, sir," he replied, his eyes widening. "Are there horses and cows?"

"Yes, there are. And I'll let you ride a horse with me if your mama says it's okay."

Cody looked hopefully at her and she nodded. "If you're with your dad," she said with only the tiniest hesitation before she said "dad." How odd it seemed to say that and mean Nick, even though it was an accurate description.

As she worked beside him, she couldn't keep from having a sharp awareness of Nick, or having fun with him and Cody. But every moment of fun with Nick fanned the fiery attraction between them and made heartache loom more threateningly. How could she protect her heart from Nick's appeal and charm when she was tied to him forever by their son?

It was midmorning when they left in the limo for the aquarium. As they walked through the building and took a train that passed between large tanks of fish, her gaze ran across Nick's broad shoulders, his narrow waist and long legs. His boots gave him height that he didn't need, and just looking at him she felt her pulse jump. Only her squealing son deflected her attention.

At one point Nick stepped close to Claire while she stood with Cody and watched fish swim past on the other side of the glass. "I've made reservations to take you both out to eat tonight. Seven o'clock. If it's too late for Cody, I can change the time."

"No, that will be fine."

She still had the afternoon to get through at the aquarium, and now dinner. How would she make it through the day without giving in to the temptation that was Nick Milan?

That evening Nick and Cody waited downstairs. Cody played with his new laptop and Nick helped him until he heard Claire's heels in the hallway. He stood and walked toward the doorway as she entered. She'd changed into a scarlet crepe dress with a scoop neckline, and her hair fell to her shoulders and was caught up slightly on each side by a tortoiseshell comb. The only jewelry she wore was the diamond necklace he had given her and the gold charm bracelet.

"You look gorgeous, Claire," Nick said in a husky drawl.

His insides knotted and he had to struggle to stop staring at her.

"Thank you. Both the men in my life look oh, so handsome," she said, smiling at Cody who wore a white dress shirt tucked neatly into black slacks.

"Thank you," Cody said dutifully.

"Thank you, also," Nick said, barely aware of his answer because Claire took all his attention. How could he get through the evening without flirting with her, touching her, kissing her?

Nick picked up Cody. "Let's go eat dinner. The limo is waiting."

Through dinner Cody was fascinated by the sparkling city lights out the window. Nick just wanted to look at Claire. In spite of the dangers to his heart, he couldn't take his attention from her. Her smooth skin looked soft, beautiful, her dark eyes wide, luminous, her sensual mouth an invitation for erotic thoughts. He nearly groaned each time his eyes lit on her. He turned, trying to focus on his son as Cody enjoyed his macaroni and cheese.

After they'd eaten their lobster dinners, Claire told him, "I looked at my calendar this afternoon, talked to my secretary and to Grandma. Cody and I can come see you next week, Nick. I think Wednesday would be good. I don't want to overstay our welcome and I need to make plane reservations. I don't want to drive."

"You don't have to drive or make plane reservations. You can fly in the Milan plane. Come on Monday, if you possibly can, and give us a whole week. We can go to the ranch and if that begins to wear thin with him, then we can all go to Dallas."

"We'll come Tuesday. I'll need to go into the office Monday and make sure things are all set for the week."

"I'll look forward to Tuesday, then."

* * *

It was nine by the time they returned home, and by ten Cody was in bed asleep.

"He likes you—which doesn't surprise me," Claire said as she walked with Nick to the family room. Nick shed his coat and tie, unbuttoning the top buttons of his shirt, making her remember the endless nights of making love with him. Beneath his tailor-made clothes was a fit, muscular male body that she could remember far too well.

She feared sitting here with him, alone. There was no telling how traitorous her own body could be. Instead, she had an idea. "C'mon, I'll give you the deluxe tour downstairs." She grabbed her iPad. "We can hear Cody on the monitor anywhere in the house."

She started the tour in the hall. "We have two suites in that wing downstairs and there's an elevator for my grandparents even though they've already moved downstairs. My grandmother still goes upstairs, but she sleeps downstairs." Claire was aware of Nick close at her side as they strolled through the downstairs. They looked at one wing and then moved to another to enter a large gym.

"Someday I'll have a pool outside, but until then, this is where I get my exercise."

"Great," Nick said, looking at the polished wood floor. "Do you have any music in here? It would be fun to move around a bit. We can dance."

For a moment she was tempted to refuse. Dancing with Nick had always been sexy. She gazed up at him, looking into blue eyes that melted her resistance.

"I have music I exercise with," she replied.

Aware of Nick standing and watching her, she turned on a tape. "Here's a good dance tape—a bit of everything."

"First, let's change something here," he said, walking to her and reaching up to take the combs out of her hair so it fell freely around her face. "That's the way I like your hair best." He dropped the combs into his pocket.

She still reacted to him as much as she had years earlier. Was it Nick, or was it simply because there hadn't been men in her life in the years in between?

"You shouldn't take down my hair, Nick," she whispered, looking at his mouth and then back to see desire flare in his blue eyes. "And we shouldn't dance."

As he inhaled deeply, he shook his head. "It's a fast song and we'll move around, which will help blow off steam," he said, but his voice was deeper and the look in his eyes clearly indicated he wanted to kiss her. Even though she knew she shouldn't, she wanted Nick's kiss.

He stepped farther back from her and began to dance to the fast beat. As they danced, she was aware of his gaze steadily on her, moving over her body and back up to hold her gaze. Dancing didn't blow off steam as he had predicted. In fact, watching his sexy moves only stirred her desire.

Still, she gave herself over to the moment. Moving with the pounding rhythm, she finally felt some of the tension ease.

It had been a good weekend, but they had put off the decisions and the discussions that would cause problems between them. For a moment they were in a dangerous limbo—getting reacquainted as he got to know his son, deliberately avoiding decisions.

The next number was a polka. Smiling, Nick took her hands to whirl around the spacious room. She hadn't danced a polka with anyone in years and she felt as if her feet barely touched the floor while she flew around the room with Nick, laughing. A ballad followed and Nick took her hand to dance, keeping a distance between them.

He grinned as they danced slowly. "Who put this playlist together?"

"I did. I like music when I exercise and I've got eclectic taste."

"I haven't danced a polka since college and that's getting to be a long time ago."

"Oh, sure. Aeons ago," she said, smiling at him.

"That's better. It's good to see you smile," he said.

"When this one is over, let's go sit and have a cool drink. I'm ready for some quiet," she said, thinking they should stop dancing and touching each other. Every contact added to her awareness of him, building the risks to her heart.

"We can go now." They stopped dancing and he waited while she turned off the music and then hit the light switch as they left the room.

"I love your home," he said. "And you've done so well with Cody. When you come to Dallas, I'd like to have my family out so they can meet him."

"That's fine, Nick. How is your family? Is Madison still painting? I met her when she had an exhibit in Houston."

"My family is fine. Madison married Jake Calhoun and she doesn't travel as much. She has the family ranch now, but lives on Jake's ranch. Wyatt is county sheriff, of all things. Friends talked him into taking the office, but he's retiring to his ranch after this term. Tony is ranching and the busy bachelor. We see each other fairly often. My folks are in Dallas and Dad is retired."

"You should break the news about Cody to your parents first. Your father will no doubt have things he wants you to do."

"Most of my life I've gotten along with Dad and I've done what he wanted. Even more than Wyatt, who never gave Dad trouble. Madison and Tony—well, that's a different story. Particularly Tony. Frankly, I don't think he was right in the way Dad dealt with Madison, but that's over and she's married to Jake Calhoun now." He shrugged. "I think Dad will cooperate with me just because we've always gotten along."

"You mean you've always done what your dad wanted."

"Yes, I have. I don't think he's been unreasonable," he said. "Dad has helped me in my career and in politics. I owe nearly everything to him. He seems to have endless contacts."

Those *endless contacts* worried her. Judge Milan was a powerful man. While Claire had never even met his parents, she suspected they didn't want Nick marrying a woman with obligations far from DC, as well as someone who would not put Nick's career first. She could understand their concern for their son's future and his happiness, but it didn't help her feelings when she had been so in love with Nick and he had seemed to be with her.

"I'll talk to my dad. Don't worry about my family," he said as they headed to her kitchen. "This is their grandson, and right now their only grandson, so they're going to welcome him and love him. I'll admit that since he's a good kid and he looks like a Milan, they will really be happy about him."

"And want you to have him all the time."

He stopped and held her back. "I promise I will not take Cody from you," he said solemnly, looking directly at her.

While she nodded, she couldn't imagine how they were going to work out sharing their son if Nick moved to Washington.

They continued to walk and within minutes they sat in the family room.

Nick turned his chair to face her, pulling it close in front of hers and to one side so he had room for his long legs. He took her hand in his. "Claire, Cody is wonderful and

I'm so happy about him. I want you to be happy to have me in his life. I know it'll be difficult for you to share him when you've been accustomed to having him all the time. As long as I can see him some, I promise we'll go slowly."

"Thank you," she said, certain that his intentions were good, but soon he would have his family pressuring him to get Cody into the Milan family. Even as she thought over their dilemma, she was aware of her hand in his as it rested on his knee.

He sat too close and his gaze was too intense, but she didn't care to tell him and let him know that his touch or his nearness had that much of an impact on her.

"We can have his name changed to Milan without a marriage. Would you be opposed to that?"

"I'll think about it. I can't give you an answer instantly," she said, withdrawing her hand from his and sipping her drink.

"All I ask on anything I suggest is that you just think about it. We're exploring possibilities, that's all. Monday I'll open a trust fund for him and a savings account. I want to be part of his life in every way I can. You've done well and it's obvious you don't need my help, but I want to share in the costs for him."

"That's fine, Nick. We don't need to go back to things I've already paid. I've been able to take care of him. But we'll share costs as we move ahead."

"Good."

He picked up a long lock of her hair and let it fall through his fingers. "Whatever we work out, it's good to be with you again," he said.

She gave him a fleeting smile, unable to say the same thing back to him. Part of her wondered whether he really meant what he said, because every moment together moved them closer to another confrontation.

Now came the part she'd been dreading. "Sooner or later," she said, "we're going to have to work out a time for him to be with you and a time for him to be with me. I'd rather work it out between us and not involve lawyers. That is, except you."

"That's fine with me. Since I am a lawyer, if you change your mind and want one, that's acceptable. I just want you and Cody happy."

"He's never been away from home at night," she said, hating that she was about to lose control.

Nick leaned closer, placing his hand over hers, holding hers lightly. "Claire, I don't want to hurt you or Cody. I meant it when I said I promise I'll work with you. I just want to share my son's life and know him."

"There are moments I can't handle looking into the future. I've had him with me constantly since he was born."

"If I do something you don't like, tell me. Promise you will and I'll promise you that I'll try to work it out. How's that?"

Nodding, she began to breathe deeply and get control.

When Nick's gaze went to her mouth, her heart missed a beat. She didn't want this reaction to him, but she couldn't keep it from happening. Physically, she responded to every look, each touch. In too many ways, she liked being with Nick, and so far he was not pressuring her about Cody, but she expected that to come.

"This has been a good weekend," he said, his voice lower than usual, as it always was when his thoughts turned to sex. "Thank you for it, Claire." Leaning close, his hands on the arms of her chair, he brushed her lips lightly, an impersonal, casual kiss, but when his lips touched hers, the moment changed.

His arm tightened around her and he looked into her eyes. As she looked at his mouth, she couldn't catch her breath. Even knowing it was folly that could only cause her trouble, she wanted his kiss. That brief contact of his lips on hers stirred desire, a longing for a kiss, for a bonding, maybe even reassurance.

"Claire," he whispered, winding his fingers in her hair behind her head as he lifted her to his lap, drew her to him for a deep, passionate kiss. His arms tightened around her, pressing her against him, and she turned, slipping her arms around his shoulders, kissing him in return while longing enveloped her. How long had it been since she'd been kissed like this? How was she going to resist him?

She kissed him, wanting him, wanting the problems gone between them and wanting to make love, to get lost in passion once again.

Thought ceased as she spiraled away in his kiss, a kiss that made her hot and shaking with desire. She clung to him, wanting him to disappear and at the same time trying to bind him to her so he would never leave her.

He shifted, turning her to cradle her against his shoulder while she held him tightly.

Finally, through the haze of desire, that nagging voice of reason spoke up and she came to her senses. She realized how kissing him was going to have her tumbling into a bigger disaster. She did not want to fall in love with him again and set herself up for another heartbreak because Nick wasn't going to change and he wouldn't give up his ambitions or his career. Not for her or for Cody. As she thought of that, she shifted away from him and moved off his lap.

"This isn't going to solve anything," she whispered, standing to walk away from him.

She glanced back to find him staring at her with a shocked look that she couldn't fathom. Had their kisses touched him on some emotional level? She doubted it and she didn't want to be taken in by Nick's smooth talk.

He was a politician, accustomed to charming people and getting what he wanted out of them. He expected to win their friendship and trust. She had been all through that and it had been heartbreak that she didn't like to recall.

"Or it might solve everything," he said gruffly, as he sat up and placed his elbows on his knees.

"I'm tied to a business here and my family. You're tied to your career in Dallas, Austin and later in DC. That isn't changing, Nick, and marriage won't make any of it go away. Any personal relationship between us will complicate our lives as it did before."

He stood and crossed the room to her. "Kisses are like dancing—sexy and great fun. No harm done."

"And on that note, we'll call it a night."

"Sure," he said, falling into step beside her as they went upstairs together and stopped at her door.

"I'm going to church in the morning," she said, gazing into his blue eyes while knowing she should walk away. "Can I leave Cody with you? I'll have his breakfast ready."

"Absolutely. Leave him with me. Good night, Claire."

"Night, Nick."

She closed her door and ran her hand across her forehead. The day had been filled with ups and downs, moments when she forgot the circumstances and just had fun. There were moments in Nick's arms when years fell away and for a few minutes she was with a sexy, desirable man who dazzled her.

But, like the flip of a coin, moments could reverse. There had been times that reminded her of the problems that loomed: dividing Cody's time between them, remembering how she had felt when she had learned of his engagement and she was pregnant with his child, and the terrible breakup that had been the worst time of all.

She got ready for bed automatically, lost in her thoughts about Nick.

Unless she guarded her heart constantly, Nick was a threat to her happiness.

Then again…she glanced at the door, thinking about him in bed across the hall. Unwanted images came of lying in his arms when he was sprawled in bed, his virile male body so breathtaking. It was impossible to keep him out of her thoughts when she was sleeping only a hall away.

She couldn't stay away from him. She couldn't be with him. What was she to do? The time was coming when she'd have to make a choice.

She knew the wrong choice could blow her future happiness.

Seven

Sunday morning Claire heard Nick just before he stepped into the kitchen. Dressed in a dark brown knit shirt and chinos, he radiated vitality as he swept into the room. He had always commanded attention wherever he went and that hadn't changed.

"Good morning," he said, smiling at her. "Good morning, Cody."

Cody smiled at him. Still wearing his blue pajamas, Cody sat eating his breakfast. The woolly toy Nick had given him was in a nearby chair along with the fuzzy monkey.

"Have you named these?" Nick asked, picking up the woolly toy.

"Monster and Mr. Monkey," Cody answered.

"Good names."

She was pleased to see Nick's smile and how easily he dealt with her son. Their son, she corrected herself.

She checked the clock. "Nick, I need to leave. If you

have any questions, Cody can probably answer them and if you need me, I have my phone."

She crossed the room to kiss Cody on the forehead. "Be good for your dad. I'll be home after church."

"Yes, ma'am," Cody said, eating another bite of oatmeal.

"Can I leave him long enough to go to the door with you?" Nick asked her.

"I'm going out the back way and yes, you can," she said.

Nick walked beside her. "Don't worry about us, Claire."

"I won't. He's got a bright dad who can handle mostly all problems and Cody is a bright little kid, so you two will be fine. I'll see you after church."

"Seems like I should kiss you goodbye," he said, startling her, and then she saw his smile and knew he teased her.

"We're both better off if you don't," she said as she left.

Nick stayed the afternoon and the three played games. He was enjoying his time with them so much that it was five o'clock by the time he had his things in the limo and turned to tell them goodbye. He picked up Cody.

"You're a wonderful boy. I love you."

"I love you, Dad," Cody said as Nick hugged him.

Claire saw the look that crossed Nick's face when the boy told him he loved him and called him "dad," and her heart felt squeezed. Nick was going to pour out his love on his son. She hoped whatever she and Nick decided, it would be a good solution for Cody.

She saw Nick give her a quick glance and then look down, but she had seen the tears in his eyes and for just an instant felt a bond with him over the love they shared for their son.

After a moment he turned to Claire. "I can't wait until

the two of you get to Dallas. This has been a wonderful weekend. Thank you."

"We'll see you Tuesday," she said, thinking that if he had kept in touch with her or even told her he was getting engaged, she would have told him about her pregnancy. For a moment the old anger she sometimes felt surfaced and she stepped away from him. She didn't want to kiss him goodbye. Now that Nick wanted her in his life again, he was pouring on the charm, but she had to remember that this was the same man who had so easily dropped her for another woman and become engaged without even letting her know. There were flashes when she regretted telling him about Cody at all and wished she had just come home to Houston without Nick knowing about his son.

As quickly as those thoughts came, she tried to shut off her resentment. Nick had lost his baby. He'd gone through hell. She wasn't heartless; she'd needed to tell him about Cody, and she knew he was going to be a wonderful dad for their son. And she couldn't deprive Cody of the right to know his father. If the Milans didn't try to take Cody or monopolize him, then they could work together. She hoped Nick's dad stayed out of it and let them work things out in their own way. Meanwhile, she had to keep her heart intact. The only way to do that was to stay out of Nick's arms…and out of his bed.

Nick settled in the limo and looked at Claire and Cody standing on the curving front walk. Claire held Cody with one hand and with the other she pushed back her hair, which swirled across her cheek in the wind.

Cody waved and Nick's heart lurched as he waved back. Cody's declaration of love, his simple, *I love you, Dad*, had wrapped around his heart and he would never forget the moment. Cody was so small, his thin arms had been around Nick's neck. He loved his son beyond measure.

I love you, Dad. Those plain words had been the greatest gift. Briefly, he thought about Claire, wishing they didn't have all the problems between them because they both loved Cody. She had given him a wonderful son. Nick tried to stop wishful thinking. The limo pulled away, driving slowly down her street. He couldn't look continually at what might have been, but it was a struggle to avoid doing so. For an instant he questioned his future. Was a political career worth losing Claire's love and missing out on becoming a husband with a loving, caring family?

He gave his head a shake, as if trying to get rid of such thoughts. Being with Claire again, he'd been caught up in desire for her that muddled his thinking.

He already missed being with both of them. Could he keep from falling in love with her and demolishing all his future plans? Could he risk another broken heart? Their problems were bigger now and chances of working them out far less likely than before.

Everything was different now. Because of Cody.

He had never dreamed how much he would love his son. Cody was a wonderful child. A lot of credit for that went to Claire and her family. He felt another big rush of gratitude and made a mental note to order flowers for her when he got home.

He couldn't wait to take Cody to the ranch on Tuesday. In the meantime, when he got home, he had to break the news to his parents first and then let his siblings know. He had to tell Karen's family at some point, too, and they weren't going to be overjoyed to learn that he had a son who was born months after he had married their late daughter.

He sent his dad a text, asking about stopping by to see

him. In minutes he received an answer to come by as soon as he returned home to Dallas. Better to face the lion in his den right away, he told himself.

Nick walked into the study, greeted his mother with a hug and crossed the room to shake hands with his dad. With their small dog jumping around his feet, Nick sat and chatted with them, talking about the weather, the basketball season.

"Evelyn," his dad said, "I need to talk to Nick for a short time. A legal matter."

She held up her hand and smiled. "No need for me to sit through a tedious discussion. I'm gone. Peter, call me when you finish," she told her husband as she walked out with the dog trotting behind her.

As soon as they were alone and the doors were closed, Nick turned to his dad. "I have something to discuss with you when you're finished."

"I don't have anything. That was just an excuse to get your mother to leave. I guessed that you came by for a reason."

"You know me pretty well," Nick said, dreading the next few minutes, knowing he and his father had different views on a lot of basic things and this was going to be one of the biggest.

Nick stood, walking to the mantel to turn and face his dad. "Dad, you remember before I got engaged to Karen, I proposed to Claire Prentiss from Houston, but she turned me down."

"I remember. Mr. Prentiss, the grandfather, had a thriving real estate business in Houston. They handled many big homes. The young woman helped her grandfather in the business."

"That's right." Nick's dread increased. He wondered

how he'd find the words to tell his father what he knew would start a fight. Then again, he told himself that once his father knew about Cody, he'd accept him.

He took a deep breath and continued. "Let's jump ahead to last week when a client asked me to go to a real estate closing with him. The seller was hospitalized and unable to attend, but they had the real estate agent fill in for her. It was Claire Prentiss. She runs her grandfather's agency now."

"I don't think you came to tell me you're dating her again."

"No, I didn't. She didn't know I had lost Karen and our baby." He could see he had his dad's full attention now. "If you recall, I broke up with Claire because we couldn't work out how we would live. She had family responsibilities and I had started a new career. Then I began dating Karen, and you and mom pushed me to marry her."

"Which I still think was good. We just couldn't foresee the drunk driver."

"I didn't tell Claire that I was engaged, but she learned about it."

His father shrugged. "Well, we're in local magazines and papers, and so is Karen's family."

"I have something I bought for you and Mom. Let me get it."

"Nick, just tell me what it is. I don't need to see it."

"You'll want to see this. Trust me." Nick crossed the room to his briefcase and removed two iPads. He remembered how all his anger had vanished when he'd seen Cody's picture. He was counting on Cody's picture having the same effect on his father.

"This iPad is for you." He put it on a table. "But for now I want to show you something on mine." He carried the tablet back to his dad, pulled a chair close and sat. "Get ready for a shock," he said, gazing into his father's eyes.

"Well, now I am curious," he said as he pushed his bifocals up.

Nick held the iPad out and his dad grasped it. "Dad, this is Cody Nicholas Prentiss. When I married Karen, Claire was pregnant with my son."

"Oh, damn, Nick." For a moment his father looked stricken and all color left his face. "You got her pregnant and then you got engaged to Karen? She didn't tell you?" he asked, looking at Nick.

"No, sir. Remember, I didn't tell her I was engaged and marrying another woman," Nick said, as his father looked down at the iPad in his hands.

He pulled the tablet and stared intently. "Damn, Nick, this child is the image of you. He's you all over again," he said in an awestruck voice. Nick let out his breath because he had a feeling that Cody had just been accepted into his father's world.

Judge Milan looked at his son. "Are you going to marry Claire?"

Nick shook his head. "I just learned about Cody last week and I just spent the weekend with her in Houston getting to know him. This family is going to love him. He is smart, happy, a great kid. He's three years old and yes, he does look like my pictures when I was that age. He's a Milan, there's no mistaking it."

His father barely looked up, still studying Cody's picture.

"Dad, I have more pictures." Nick swiped the screen and scrolled through other pictures of Cody laughing at the camera.

"Nick, we've got to break this gently to your mother, but she is going to want this little boy in her life in the worst way." His dad looked up. "This is our first and only grandchild, Nick. And he couldn't look more like a Milan."

Nick was so relieved, but at the same time, he knew his dad's acceptance meant his parents were going to fight to get Cody into the family. Nick glanced around the room, remembering being in the same room while his dad had argued and pressured him to marry Karen and forget Claire. Nick made a silent vow to himself that when Cody was grown, he'd never interfere in his life the way his dad had interfered in his own.

"I've invited Claire to bring Cody to Dallas this week. She'll be here Tuesday and I'm taking them out to my ranch. One night while they're here I thought I'd have the family over to meet him."

"You've got to marry her, Nick. The sooner the better."

"At this point she isn't interested in marrying me. Her grandfather isn't well. Her mother has passed away and her grandmother is getting older. Claire has control of the real estate business totally and she's been very successful and built it up. She has three offices and seventy employees in Houston, and she doesn't want to leave there. She's built a big, fine mansion in an exclusive area, and Cody and her grandmother live with her. Her grandfather is in assisted living, but she hopes to bring him home. She told me there have been no other men in her life because she hasn't had time for a social life, and I can see that." The words rushed out, like an eruption. But he wanted to lay everything out on the table right away.

He wondered whether his father even heard him; he was still going through the pictures. He reminded himself that his dad could do two things at once and not miss a word of conversation around him.

Finally his father looked up. "Go get your mother. You can tell her when you get in here where she can see his picture. I know why you showed it to me first. Nick, can you print a couple of these out for us, so we can keep some?"

"I asked Claire to print a few out, so I have some for you. But, Dad, that's why I'm giving you an iPad. I've already loaded all those pictures on it for you and Mom to look at."

"That's dandy, Nick. That's just fine. Thank you," his father said, his gaze returning to Cody's picture. "Our first grandchild," he said with awe in his voice. "Three years—damn, if only we had known."

"You know why we didn't." Nick couldn't keep from saying and his father waved his hand at him without looking up. "Go get your mother. She is going to be so happy over this. Nick, we've never even met Claire."

"No, Dad, you haven't, but you will this week." Clinging to his patience he bit back pointing out that they hadn't wanted to meet Claire. "I'll get Mom."

His mother looked puzzled when she returned and Judge Milan motioned her to come sit beside him. He took her hand. "Nick has some good news that will surprise you as well as shock you."

Nick went through telling her in the same way he had told his father.

"Oh, my word, you fathered a child out of wedlock!" his mother said, frowning and sounding devastated. Then, before he could respond, her eyes grew soft. "We have a grandchild." Then she stared at the iPad.

He gave her a moment to digest it all.

"Oh, my word, Nick. This is a picture of you."

"No, it's my son and Claire is his mother," Nick said. "His name is Cody Nicholas."

"She gave him your name." Evelyn didn't look up from the pictures as she spoke. "He's definitely your son. We're grandparents and we get to meet him this week?" His mother's voice filled with excitement. She looked up at Nick. "I'm a grandmother. Oh, Nick, I'm so thrilled."

"I'm glad, Mom," he said.

It was another hour before he was ready to leave. He left the iPad with pictures of Cody with them and said he would arrange for a family dinner on whatever night they could get the most members of the family together. As he kissed his mother's cheek and started out of the room, his dad got up.

"I'll walk you to the car, Nick," he said, catching up with Nick.

Nick wasn't surprised. He knew his father had a purpose in walking him to the car.

As soon as they were out of the house, his dad cleared his throat. "Nick, think about asking Claire to marry you. She may be wealthy, comfortable, successful, but she doesn't have the wealth our family does. You can give her a sum that would win the cooperation of most any woman and you can set up a trust fund for Cody, plus give him the Milan name. That will be difficult for her to turn down."

"Dad, I hurt her badly once. I don't want to do it again. If I'd done what I should have in the first place, I would have known about Cody. But that's in the past now. I'm not going to coerce her into marriage."

"It isn't coercion to offer what I'm talking about. It's a fabulous, life-altering gift. Be smart about this, Nick. You have the highest political ambitions and we're getting a lot of powerful people lined up to support you. Don't blow this now. That little boy is a Milan, our grandchild. I can't tell you how thrilled your mother and I both are."

"I'm glad for that. You're going to be more thrilled when you meet him. He's adorable."

"Nick, if she would marry you, it would kill any breath

of scandal attached to Cody. Think about it," his dad urged, giving him one of his patented looks.

"Sure. I will," Nick answered. "I'll let my siblings know about him as soon as I get home. I'm going to let Karen's parents know too. Mom is probably already on the phone talking to Madison."

"She won't talk to any of the family until she's talked to me again." They stopped beside Nick's car and his father looked up at him. "Just think about what I said. It would help your political chances to be married with a family."

"I will." Nick climbed behind the wheel. "Night, Dad. I'll be in touch."

"Thanks for the iPad. This is an exciting night in our lives. We have a grandson. That's marvelous, Nick. I'm looking forward to meeting him and his mother."

Nodding, Nick felt a pang. He had gotten his life into a muddle, cutting Claire out of it, then losing Karen and the baby. And now it was even more mixed-up.

He drove to his Dallas home and went inside. He called Wyatt first, telling him about Cody and sending a picture. He did the same with Madison and then Tony.

Feeling Karen's parents should know, he called and talked to her dad briefly. To his relief, her father seemed happy for Nick to have a child. He realized a lot of despair over his loss was fading.

Then he called Claire. She was putting Cody to bed, but Nick got to talk to him for ten minutes. Just hearing his voice nearly brought tears to his eyes; he missed his son so much already. He could hardly wait till Tuesday. Claire promised to call Nick after she was finished with Cody.

He wondered what she thought. She kept everything bottled up and put a barrier between them. He understood why she did, and he knew he should, too, for the same reasons.

Was the career he had planned really better than having Claire's love and Cody in his life?

Somehow over the weekend, politics had lost a bit of its luster.

Giving up political office was a thought that had never crossed his mind before, and he couldn't imagine changing his whole way of life and giving up his ranch to move to Houston. He would never be happy. That thought was followed by memories of this weekend, which had been one of the happiest times of his life. How much would becoming a father change his life? And change his feelings for Claire?

He got out his iPad and looked at all of Cody's pictures again. He'd already received text messages from his siblings, congratulating him and telling him how much Cody looked like Nick and like the Milans, and responding to his invitation to meet Claire and Cody.

By consensus it'd be Saturday night when he'd host the party at his Dallas home. He could hardly wait.

Tuesday Nick went to the airport to meet Claire and Cody. He had taken little time off for two years and his office was accustomed to being able to get in contact with him during all hours. That was going to have to change and it would be a big adjustment in his life.

He was eager to see them, surprised how the anticipation had kept him awake all night. They'd been in his thoughts constantly from yesterday until now. His life had not been empty—or, at least, he hadn't thought it was—but excitement gripped him now as he watched the plane land. It was an excitement he hadn't ever felt. Not even with his late wife. In his own way, he'd loved Karen, but he realized now that what they'd had was more like a marriage of convenience. She had done what she wanted and he had been free to pursue his career for hours on end. Setting those thoughts aside to be examined at a later time, he focused on Claire and their son.

When they emerged from the plane, his heart skipped a beat as he looked at Claire. Wearing a black knee-length coat with a thick fur collar and cuffs, black slacks and black heels, she looked like a model. A cold December wind blew, causing her hair to swirl across her cheek. She still could set his pulse racing and capture his attention far too easily for his own good. Cody was almost bouncing with each step and Nick suspected the boy was wound up with excitement. Wearing a bright blue parka and khakis, he held his tiger under one arm and the monkey under the other.

Nick walked out to meet them and picked up Cody and gave him a hug. "I'm so glad to see you," he said, carrying him and smiling at him. Cody grinned in return, wrapping one thin arm around Nick's shoulder.

"I've been counting the minutes," Nick said lightly.

"So has he. The plane was as big a hit as the limo," she said, smiling up at Nick. "He's so excited. This is all new to him. We don't travel. That's one thing about the real estate business—it's better business if I stay home."

"That I know. You look great, Claire."

"Thanks. Grandma said to thank you again. She really appreciated your call and asking her yourself to come with us. Thanks also from me."

"I'd be happy to have her here to meet my family."

"I take it your dad adjusted."

Laughing, Nick nodded. "I took a lesson from you and put Cody's picture in front of him as I told him. My parents are overcome with delight at being grandparents. To them, Cody looks just like me at that age and they are ecstatic. I haven't seen them like this many times in my life. They can't wait to meet you, too."

She nodded but her smile never reached her eyes. He knew she was worried and wished there was something he could do to alleviate her concern.

"They can't wait to see Cody. If it's acceptable with you, we'll stop by for just a few minutes. I promise we won't stay."

"That's fine. We're here for your family to get to know Cody, so see any of them you want. They're his grand-parents, Nick."

"Thanks," he said, wondering how she truly felt toward all of them. "They're all happy to learn about Cody and they all think he looks like me, which of course, I like to hear." When they climbed into the limo, they both focused on Cody, who seemed as interested in the interior as he'd been on the first ride.

At his parents' home, the driver slowed to park at the front door on the wide circular drive. Wearing their coats, his parents waited on the porch and came forward to greet them.

"Claire, meet my parents, Judge Peter Milan and Eve-lyn Milan. Mom and Dad, this is Claire Prentiss and this is our son and your grandson, Cody Nicholas Prentiss."

Cody shyly said hello and put his hand out to shake hands with Judge Milan. Nick knew his father would be impressed.

His mom hugged Claire lightly. "This is the most special moment," she said, dabbing at her eyes, and Nick wondered how Claire felt. Too many times he could not read her ex-pression and this was another one of those times because she had that cool, shuttered look, as if she had locked away her feelings and was going through the motions.

"It's nice for Cody to know his family," Claire said.

"You can't imagine how much he looks like Nick did at that age," Evelyn said.

"Welcome to the family," Peter Milan said, extending his hand to Claire.

"Thank you, Judge Milan," Claire said, smiling at him, another cool smile that kept up a barrier, but Nick doubted if his father realized it. "It's Cody whom I hope you'll welcome into the family."

"We're thrilled beyond anything you can imagine," he said easily. "And what a fine boy he is. Hard to realize he's just three years old because he acts older."

"He's with adults all the time," Claire answered.

"Come inside. I hear you've built up that business your grandfather had to an impressive size," Judge Milan said to her.

Nick knew his dad could pour on the charm when he wanted. With a twinge of amusement he wondered how happily his parents would have accepted a rowdy little boy who looked like Claire and bore no resemblance to the Milans. He suspected it might have made very little difference, because they were almost deliriously happy to have a grandchild. He knew his mother had been devastated by Karen's death, but now he realized a lot of her grief had included the tiny baby Nick had lost.

They sat in the less formal family room and Nick was certain it was for Cody's benefit because this room had always been childproof. His father sat close to Claire, and Nick was certain that his dad was determined to win her friendship.

"Cody," Nick's mother said, "we have a present for you." From one side of her chair she picked up a big box that was wrapped and tied in a huge red bow.

Cody's eyes sparkled, but before he moved he glanced

at Claire, who nodded, and only then did he cross the room to open his present.

"Mama, look," Cody said, holding up a magic kit. He removed the big, black top hat and put it on his head. He smiled at Evelyn Milan. "Thank you very much."

"You're welcome, Cody."

He turned to the judge. "Thank you, sir."

"Cody, come here," Judge Milan said. When Cody walked over, he leaned forward and gave him a level look. "I'd like you to think about what you want to call us, and talk to your mama and daddy about it. We're your grandparents, so we need to get the right name."

"Yes, sir," Cody said, looking at Nick.

"We'll figure that one out later, Cody. Now, come look at your magic box," Nick said.

Cody ran back to the box to rummage in it and pull out the cape, which he put on.

Evelyn clapped. "Excellent, Cody. You look like a magician. You need your magic wand," she said.

They spent an hour with his parents before Nick asked Cody to put away his magic kit because they needed to go.

As they drove away, his parents stood waving and Claire and Cody waved in return. "I think they matched my own family's enthusiasm for Cody," Claire said.

"Believe me, it's sincere. It's beyond anything I dreamed. Whatever we work out in the future, you and Cody have instantly become members of the family, so I hope you like the Milans."

"I've met Madison. I haven't met Tony or Wyatt."

"The whole world likes Wyatt. He's quiet, but not as quiet as he used to be before he married. You'll like Tony, too. They all want to meet Cody. Just now with my folks, Cody was a hit, which I knew he would be. Mom would have loved him no matter what, unless he had been a hellion, but my dad was impressed and so pleased. I know how to read the signs."

"The magic kit is a hit, that's for sure. You can teach him the tricks."

"Claire, I've been counting the minutes. I'm glad you're here. We'll go by my house, eat lunch there and then fly to the ranch in Verity. We can do a little shopping before we leave Verity—get Cody some cowboy clothes. He doesn't have any boots, does he?"

"No, he doesn't and he'll be thrilled. You're doing all the right things."

"I want to do all the right things for his mom, too," Nick said.

"You're doing pretty good at that, too," she said, but her voice sounded somber, as if she wished he wouldn't bother trying to please her. Was she still angry with him? Or was she just trying to avoid getting friendly enough to fall in love again? He had no idea what Claire's thoughts were. She had a big part of herself locked away, causing him to worry about their dealings. He knew his dad was going to push him to marry Claire. Now he just had to keep his dad from trying to push Claire, because that would only make matters worse.

They went to Nick's house and when they arrived he gave them a tour. The house was only slightly larger than Claire's, set back on a lot with tall trees, fountains in front of the house, a spacious patio and a fenced area with a swimming pool in the back. "Claire, I've had an alarm installed in the pool and it already had a fence. If anything over a few pounds goes into the pool, the alarm will sound. So there's no way Cody can wander out there and fall in without us knowing."

She stared at the pool that was surrounded by a high, iron fence. She turned to him.

"Thanks, Nick, I feel much better about that because he'll be with you sometimes when I'm not and that's one worry I won't have."

"I don't want you to have any worries about Cody being with me," Nick said, glancing at his son who was digging through his box of magic tricks as they stood in an informal sitting room that overlooked the patio.

"I have a staff, but I've given them the rest of this week off since we're going to the ranch—at least, they're off until Saturday when we return. My cook and the head of my cleaning staff are at the ranch today. There should be lunch left here for us," he said. "I'll get it on, and after we eat we'll fly to Verity."

"I'll help. Cody is happy with his present."

As soon as they stepped into his kitchen she stopped. "Nick, when did you get the booster seat for Cody?"

"I called my secretary and told her what I needed and she ordered it for me. It'll do, won't it?"

"Of course, it'll do," Claire said, smiling, and Nick couldn't resist moving closer.

"At least it got a smile out of you and that makes it worth the expense and trouble. Claire, I want this to be good from your viewpoint, too."

Her smile disappeared as she gazed intently at him. "I'm trying to cooperate and I know we have to work something out between us. You've been good, and believe me, I appreciate it."

He hugged her lightly, trying to give her an impersonal, casual hug of reassurance that he meant what he said and he hoped to avoid hurting her. But the moment she was in his arms, he became aware of her soft curves pressed against him, of the exotic perfume she wore that was the faintest of scents, yet enticing. Locks of her silky hair touched his cheek. Desire swept him, sudden and unexpected, shaking him to his core. He stood still, trying to keep control. He thought back on how they used to flirt, tease each other and have fun together. That was gone. Now he intended to keep her from worrying and to be friendly with her. And "friendly" meant no kissing.

He stepped away. "Okay?"

"Sure, Nick."

"I mean, am I okay? I'm trying to do what you'd like."

"You're fine," she said, giving him a smile that made him feel better.

"Let's get lunch on before a hungry kid shows up."

"With that magic kit he won't think about food for another hour. Food comes way down on his list of fascinating things in life."

After holding her close, wanting to kiss her, Nick was acutely aware of her moving around him, brushing past him, their hands meeting as she handed him a dish. This week would be wonderful in so many ways, but tense and difficult in others. He needed to remember to resist Claire, as well as guard his heart. Could he do that when he would be with her constantly?

Eight

Claire looked out the plane window at the rolling land spread below. Mesquite trees, some brown, some still a dull, winter green, were bent by the prevailing south winds coming across Texas from the Gulf of Mexico. It was a view different from the area around Houston.

She glanced at Nick, who was poring over the magic book with Cody while Cody held a string of brightly colored scarves tied together and tried to stuff them into the hat. She never dreamed how much his family would like Cody and like being grandparents.

It was also easy to see that Judge Milan wanted her to marry Nick and wanted it badly. She could imagine he saw her as the perfect wife now for Nick. Marrying would smooth away any scandal about Cody's birth and help Nick in his career. She suspected Judge Milan would start his campaign to sway her as soon as possible.

But for Claire, the most worrisome thing was her intense physical reaction to Nick. When he had taken her into his arms for just a casual hug, her heart thudded and her breath caught. Seduction would only add to their problems and she intended to guard against it, even though it seemed to grow more difficult each hour she spent with Nick.

"Here's Verity," Nick said when the plane banked and she saw a town below.

She gazed out the window at this town she had heard about, but had only been through without stopping when Nick had taken her to his family's ranch years earlier. At that time he didn't have his own ranch, but the family ranch had been vacant the weekend they went, so they had it to themselves and Nick had been far more relaxed than any other time she had been with him.

Shortly, they rode in Nick's car down a wide street. In downtown Verity Christmas lights and wreaths were strung on lampposts and it seemed as if the whole town was decorated for the holidays. Nick parked at the back of the sheriff's office and they went inside where a small, lighted Christmas tree stood in the lobby.

They waited until the sheriff came to the front, and the minute she saw the man's blue eyes and brown hair, so like Nick's and Cody's, she knew he had to be a Milan. This was Wyatt, she realized. His features were far more rugged than Nick's, who had the appealing looks of a handsome movie star.

Wyatt's ready smile was as inviting as his brother's. "It's really good to meet you, Claire. I've heard about you and now about Cody. I'm an uncle. Wow." He turned to shake hands with Cody, who looked awed by Wyatt's uniform.

"This is your Uncle Wyatt, Cody," Nick said. "He's the sheriff."

"Cody, would you like to look around?" Wyatt asked. "Want to see the jail?"

Cody nodded, and Claire smiled because for one of the rare moments in his life, her son was suddenly shy. Nick took Cody's hand. "C'mon, we'll look at the jail."

"As thrilling as that is going to be," Claire said, "I'll leave the males to tour and I'll go shopping. Nick, I have my phone and you have my number. Wyatt, where's a good store for jeans?"

"Try The Plaza. I'm not the best to ask about women's jeans." He turned to one of his officers seated behind a desk. "Dwight?"

"The Plaza is a good one. So is Dorothy's."

"There you go," Wyatt said, and smiled. "Dwight will give you directions. When you're through, meet us at the drugstore across the street next door to the hotel. I'll get Cody a soda if he wants one and if that's all right?"

"Yes, it is with me. You can ask him if he wants one."

She left as she heard Cody say, "Yes, sir."

All the time she tried on jeans, she was aware she would be wearing them around Nick. On impulse, she bought a shirt to match.

It was over an hour later when she entered the drugstore to find the men and Cody seated at a round table in old-fashioned ice-cream-parlor chairs. A fire burned in a potbellied stove in the center of the big room and a lighted Christmas tree stood in the window. As she walked to them, she was aware of Nick's steady gaze on her. He came to his feet along with Wyatt.

"Please be seated," she said. "Looks as if everyone's had a soda."

"Best in the West," Nick said, smiling. "Love these sodas. Can I get you one?"

"I'll pass, but thank you. Cody, are they really the best?"

"Yes, ma'am," he said, licking his lips and everyone laughed. "Mama, Uncle Wyatt gave me a badge." Cody turned in his chair and she leaned down to look at a gold star that resembled Wyatt's badge and said Verity Junior Sheriff.

"That's great. I hope you thanked him."

"I did," Cody said as he shot a big grin Wyatt's way.

She smiled at Wyatt, too. "Uncle Wyatt, you're already on his favorite relative list, I'm sure."

"I hope so," Wyatt answered easily.

"Dad bought me boots and a hat," Cody said.

"Well, you will be all fixed up with your boots and junior sheriff badge and hat," she said, certain Cody would love every minute of this trip. Even though Cody's reasons would be far more simple, was she going to be pressured by her son to marry Nick?

They sat and talked for another half hour until Nick pushed back his chair. "I think we'll head to the ranch now, Wyatt."

They walked back to the sheriff's office and in minutes Nick was driving south out of Verity.

As Nick wound up the drive to the sprawling ranch house, she wondered about his life. "Do you ever stay out here, Nick?"

"Not much. I don't have time to, but someday I hope to retire early and live here because I love it. Ranching is ingrained in our family. You can't pry my youngest brother Tony off his ranch. Wyatt loves it and will go back to living on his ranch when his term as sheriff ends. He took on that job as a favor to a lot of people, but that's not his deal. Madison lives on a ranch now with her husband, Jake Calhoun, but before she married Jake, she lived on the family ranch a good part of the year and painted there. We all love the cowboy life."

"I'd think you'd arrange a little more time for it, then. If you can't work this into your life, how are you going to fit Cody in?" she asked, wondering whether Nick was actually going to want much time with Cody when they got right down to figuring out a schedule.

With a quick glance, Nick gave her a startled look. "I'll try to give Cody top priority," Nick answered. His voice was quiet, his tone somber. Was he just facing reality about how much time his political career would take away from a family?

She looked at his profile, his firm jaw, prominent cheekbones, handsome features, thickly lashed eyes. Nick was the best-looking Milan of all those she had met. Probably the best-looking man she had ever met at all. Or was she biased because of personal feelings? She couldn't answer her own question.

In the warm car she had opened her coat. Now she touched the heart pendant Nick had given her. "My necklace is beautiful," she said. "Thank you again."

"It's just a token thank-you for Cody. You should have had more."

"Nick, this has over twenty-four big diamonds. It's more than a token," she said, wondering whether he had given it to her out of gratitude or guilt.

"I promise you, that's a token for what I feel I should give you. Here we are," he said, stopping the car near the back door of a sprawling ranch house with an inviting porch. They each carried bags inside and Cody brought his toys. "C'mon, and I'll show you where your rooms will be," Nick said. "I can bring in the rest of the stuff later."

They walked into a spacious kitchen with stainless steel state-of-the-art equipment. Nick had dark fruitwood cabinets and woodwork with pale yellow walls and floor to ceiling windows overlooking the lawn along one wall and the patio on the other. Standing at the sink was a tall white-haired man who turned to smile at them.

"Claire, meet Douglas Giroux, my cook, who's worked

for me a long time now. Zelda, his wife, heads my cleaning staff," Nick said. "Douglas works for me in Dallas, but he agreed to come out here for these few days. Douglas, this is Miss Prentiss and my son, Cody."

"Welcome to the ranch," Douglas said. "I hope you enjoy your stay."

"Something you're cooking smells inviting," Nick said.

"That's a casserole to freeze. Tonight we'll have creamed pheasant, baked potatoes, asparagus and rolls."

"Sounds wonderful," Claire said, as Nick took her arm to walk down the hall. The casual touch sent a tingling current down her spine. No matter how much she decided to avoid responding to him, her body couldn't get the message. She struggled to focus on the house instead of the tall man at her side.

He led her to her bedroom for the week, done in bright colors with white furniture. Cody's room adjoined it and held a junior bed and a big white stuffed bear that Cody ran to hug the minute he walked into the room.

"That's for you, Cody," Nick said, smiling at his son.

"Thank you," Cody said, beaming as he hugged the bear again.

"My room is at the end of the hall," Nick said. "You're welcome to come see it."

"Thanks. I'll unpack instead," she said. She needed some time away from this man, to regroup.

Through dinner and playing with Cody afterward, Nick was far more aware of Claire than before. Being together at the ranch had brought memories tumbling back, making love to her, holding her naked in his arms, kissing her for hours. Grief was leaving him along with the numbness. Without wanting to, she stirred memories and desire. He wanted to kiss her, to dance with her, to make love with her.

The past weekend and this week were so totally unlike his life—all business appointments put off, his calendar cleared to meet Cody and be with him. He had turned off his cell phone, knowing his family could get him through the ranch number or his foreman. The ranch was a world of its own and insulated from the outside world. He expected his life to shift back into its usual groove when he returned to work, but this was a reprieve that he would relish. He hadn't spent enough time here over the last couple of years, and certainly not during the last year of his marriage to Karen. She had never cared for the ranch. She was meant for a social life, just as his mother preferred Dallas, and that had fit with his schedule. He had forgotten just how much he loved this place. Life would be ideal here with Claire and Cody.

The idea startled him. He had a busy, important career, a career that was vital to his family and could grow more demanding in the coming years. The ranch was an idyll, he reminded himself, and there was no way he could move to the ranch now, nor would Claire ever come with him. She would not leave the big business she had built and she wouldn't leave her family. He'd best remember that.

After putting Cody to bed, Claire returned to the family room to sit with him. Her red slacks and red sweater, which clung to tempting curves, rekindled longing, making him want to untie the scarf that held her hair and let it fall loose about her shoulders, but he resisted.

"Cody's asleep. It's been an exciting day for him, Nick. His first plane ride, his first pair of boots and his first cowboy hat. His first meeting with a real sheriff. He has met new grandparents. So many things that he's dazzled by them."

Despite his good intentions, Nick took her hand, running his thumb lightly over the back of her hand. "Now I think it's time for his mom to be dazzled."

What did he mean by that? Claire wondered as she felt her pulse race.

"You've been good about all this, Claire," he said, his voice suddenly huskier. "When you get home, go out with me. Whatever works out between us, hopefully, we're going to be friends. Let me take you out for dinner—a 'just friends' thing."

She forced a smile. "I'm tempted, Nick, but I think we should avoid that kind of evening. We've been in limbo, getting you and Cody acquainted. There have been no problems, no tomorrows. We're headed for some major decisions and major upheavals in my life, Cody's life and my family's lives. Cody will be all right with what we do, but you and I won't. There is no way to work out a wonderful, happy solution to sharing him between Washington, DC and Houston. It's an upheaval for me to share him at all."

"We might fall in love if you'd give us half a chance."

The hurt she felt stabbed deeper. "You'll be so busy with your career, I think that's impossible. I'm busy with my career and my family. All I see is more heartbreak, so I don't think dinners out together will help unless it's something we need to do involving Cody. After this week, you've broken the ice and we can move on and begin to make decisions. I think the less you and I see of each other, the better we'll each be."

Aware Nick was unaccustomed to defeat of any kind, she gazed into his penetrating blue eyes. She couldn't read his reaction or even guess what he was thinking, except that she was certain he was not happy about her answer.

"If that's what you want," he finally said. "Neither of us wants another heartbreak. I can't deal with another one, but I didn't see dinner leading to that. I've been so happy this past week that everything looks rosy."

"I'm glad, Nick, but we have a lot to work out between us."

He nodded. "If we don't go to dinner, I still would like to spend some time next week with Cody. I want to see him again. Pick a time. I can stay in Houston at a hotel and keep him there with me or just come see him each day and take him out."

"That would probably work best at this point. Eventually, I know we'll have to work out a regular arrangement, but please, not this soon."

He nodded. "I'll come Tuesday and stay at a hotel and you'll barely see me."

"I think that's best," she said, hurting all over and knowing even bigger hurts were coming.

"Want something to drink before we eat? I'm having a beer."

"Just ice water."

When he got up to get the drinks, she looked around, seeing some family pictures in a frame. Her eyes were drawn to one in particular—a shot of Nick and his brothers and their father. She remembered what he'd told her about the men in his family. "Nick, you've told me about the Milan family legend that each male had to go into the field of law or his family faced disaster."

"It was never clear what kind of disaster, and I don't think we were all pushed toward law because of the legend as much as Dad wanting us in that field since he loved it. The legend goes back too far for anyone to have heard about a time it didn't exist or how it got started."

"You sort of made light of it, but your dad, your brothers and you all studied law. If I remember correctly, your youngest brother was a practicing lawyer."

He walked over with their drinks. "Tony? Yeah, for about ten minutes. He got a law degree, graduated, went to work for a law firm for one year, quit and moved back to his ranch and there he is and he will always be." He shrugged. "It's an old legend, but I don't give it much credence. I don't think any Milan really does any longer. Madison was always talented in art and no one has ever pushed any of the females into law."

"That's good to hear. I wondered whether you would be pushing Cody someday to go to law school."

"Never. Cody can do what he wants. My dad wanted us to be lawyers, but it wasn't because of that legend." Nick squeezed her hand lightly and smiled at her. "Don't give that another thought. I promise, no pushing from me to get Cody to study law because of a legend or any other reason."

"That makes me feel better. You're his dad and you're in his life now, so I'm glad to hear your views on it."

"We've had some family legends that have come true. I guess some are based on fact, but no one knows the history of this Milan legend. Probably originated by a Calhoun to cause trouble."

Knowing he was joking, she smiled. "The old feud ought to be dying."

"For some of us, that Milan-Calhoun feud is out of date and should end. Madison has married a Calhoun and so has Wyatt. Wyatt's wife is from another branch of the Calhoun family. You'll meet Milans and Calhouns at the family gathering Saturday night. If anyone keeps the feud alive, it's Tony, who fights with his Calhoun neighbor."

"I'm looking forward to Saturday night. Wyatt was a hit today with Cody. He wanted to wear his badge to bed, but I was afraid it would stick him. He thought Uncle Wyatt was super."

"What kid wouldn't? He's a sheriff. Much more exciting than my profession."

"I have to agree with you on that one."

Nick grinned at her. "I walked into that, didn't I?"

She laughed. "Even in the winter it's beautiful out here, Nick. The sunset was gorgeous. Now I know why you love to come to the ranch."

"I do," he said. "I just don't have time for it." He turned to look at her, and the look he gave her told her she was in trouble.

He couldn't resist her any longer. He'd been trying to rein himself in all day, but he was losing the battle. "Claire." He turned his chair and moved closer, reaching over to pick her up and place her on his lap. "This has been such a good day. I want to hold you," he said in a deep voice.

He heard her intake of breath. "Nick, you're borrowing trouble," she whispered, placing her hands against his chest as if she intended to push him away, but she applied no pressure.

He slipped his arm around her waist and drew her closer, his gaze going to her mouth. As he took her hand he could feel her pulse race and his jumped. He leaned closer and gave in to the temptation. He kissed her.

Her hands slipped up his chest and around his neck. She clung to him and kissed him back, and he leaned over her, kissing her hard, letting go pent-up longings, kissing her as he had wanted to since she had stepped off the plane.

He could feel her heart pounding now. He shifted to cradle her against his shoulder and poured himself into kissing her, wanting to feel alive, to make her respond the way she used to respond to him.

Her soft moan set him ablaze. She hadn't stopped him

as he thought she might. Far from it. Instead she kissed him passionately, her fingers winding in the hair at the back of his neck. Gone were her coolness, the resentment over the past. For a moment they were simply a man and woman physically drawn to each other, wanting to feel alive and good with each other once again.

He knew he was racing into disaster, but he didn't want to stop kissing her. He felt as if he could kiss her all night. He wanted to hold her, love her, seduce her. He wanted to make love to her through the night. The realization shocked him. How had she reached him? He had shut out the world, kept his attention and life focused on only business. Suddenly Claire was in his life again, turning his world upside down and making him want love in his life once more, making him want to really live again. She was burning away his grief.

They had hurt each other long ago and this might be rushing into that same hurt again, only a lot worse this time. He should stop and walk away right now, but she was soft, hot, tempting, her scalding kisses stirring a storm of longing. Life was empty without love, and the thought startled him because his life was busy every waking moment. Since when had it become empty to him? The question left him as he tightened his arms around her and continued kissing her.

Their past couldn't be undone, but they could pick up and go on with life. And it could be good again. So good.

Nick shifted her against him, wanting to carry her to a bedroom but afraid she would stop him. As he kissed her, he ran his hand lightly along her throat, caressing her, taking his time, and then his fingers drifted lower, following her luscious curves, over the softness of her breast. He twisted open a button and then another, sliding his hand beneath her blouse to touch her warm silken skin, to caress her breast, feeling the taut bud. He was aroused, ready and aching for her. He unfastened the clasp of her bra, slipping his hand below the lace to stroke her breasts with feathery touches.

She moaned, shifting her hips and moving against him, setting him on fire with wanting her.

"Nick," she whispered, sitting up. He pushed open her blouse and leaned down to touch her breast with his tongue.

She gasped and for a moment didn't stop him while he kissed and caressed her. He felt her fingers run through his hair as she moaned softly with pleasure.

"Nick, wait. A few more minutes and I won't be able to stop," she said, her words breathless. "This isn't what I planned and I don't think it's what you intended."

Reluctantly, he straightened. "Claire, I want you," he whispered, caressing her nape. He didn't want to stop touching her. "Do you remember our times together? They were better than anything. Remember?" he asked, framing her face with his hands and staring at her.

"Yes, I remember," she replied, "but we're not going there tonight. We have all the complications in our lives we need. We have to stop this." She wiggled to stand and he helped her, doing what she wanted because he wanted her happy.

He stood, looking at her while she pulled her blouse together. "I want to make love to you all night long. Making love is good between us. I know you remember. One time wouldn't hurt. We won't fall in love."

"One time wouldn't hurt," she repeated. "You're saying that to convince yourself as well as me. We hurt each other terribly before and we can't do that again."

They stood staring at each other and he wanted her desperately. He wound his hands in the thick, black hair on either side of her head, turning her head up slightly so he could get to her mouth as he leaned down to kiss her.

The minute their lips and tongues met, he wrapped his arm around her waist, pulled her tightly against him and kissed her passionately, once again letting her feel the pent-up hunger he felt. "Claire, damn, I want you," he whispered and kissed away any answer she might have had.

Moaning, she clung to him. How long they kissed, he didn't know, but finally, she pushed against him, so he released her and she stepped away. Her blouse was still unbuttoned, revealing her tempting curves, and he ached to draw her back into his embrace.

Both of them were breathing deeply and she took another step back. "Nick, we need to call it a night now. That shouldn't have even happened."

"No one was harmed. No promises made, nothing changed," he said. But his whole world had changed. He wanted her and he felt headed for more hurt than ever. He couldn't survive a marriage of convenience, which she didn't want anyway. "Claire, don't have regrets. You've brought me out of grief. For the first time in far too long, I feel alive. Don't have regrets about kissing me tonight."

"I should go to my room. That will be better for both of us."

"Sit and talk. I'll sit across the room if it'll make you happier," he said, crossing to the other side of the room.

He looked at her, his eyes pleading with her not to walk away.

Shaking her head in surrender, she acquiesced. She sat a safe distance away and he took it as a good sign that she hadn't run to her room.

For the next hour or so he forced his libido back into hiding and he gave her what she wanted—time together to talk. They talked about their families, their lives over the past few years, and Nick kept the conversation lively so he wouldn't recall how much he wanted her. He was charming, personable, trying to please her. And he succeeded.

Time slipped away until she finally stood. "I have to get to bed. I'm exhausted. Good night."

"I'll go upstairs, too," he said, crossing the room and walking with her to her door where he turned to face her.

"I'm glad you're here," he said, toying with a lock of her hair. "Both of you. Today has been really great."

"Let's hope things stay that way," she said.

Stepping closer, Nick wrapped his arms around her to kiss again, another passionate kiss that she returned. Her response was instant, intense, and it made him think she wanted him almost as much as he wanted her.

She finally looked up at him. "We're going to say good-night, Nick. I'll see you in the morning."

"This has been a very special day. Thanks for letting it happen. I'll see you and Cody early in the morning."

Nick went to his room. As he undressed, he wondered whether he would get any sleep at all this night. He lay in the dark and knew he wouldn't. Every time he closed his eyes he remembered what it was like to kiss her.

Nine

Claire gave up on sleep. She was on fire still from Nick's kisses and his caresses. She wanted to be in his arms, while at the same time she wished she hadn't let any of it happen because kisses could only complicate their relationship. They were getting over the past, building a relationship in the present. They didn't need lust complicating their lives.

She should have stopped Nick much sooner tonight, but she couldn't. Even though she knew she shouldn't, she had wanted his touch, wanted to hold him. Now sleep was gone, and once again their relationship had changed. No matter how either of them tried to deny it, the spark between them was still there, had never been extinguished. They could no longer deny the passion that shadowed every moment they would spend together. Everything would be different between them now.

How was she going to get through this time with Nick? Could she manage to just see him when she had to?

How would she get through this long night without him?

* * *

Wednesday morning after her shower she dressed in jeans, a black knit shirt and tennis shoes. Cody was still curled in bed asleep.

When she entered the kitchen, Nick was cooking and the tempting aroma of hot coffee and hot bread filled the air.

Her heart jumped as she looked at him. A blue plaid long-sleeved shirt covered his broad shoulders and was tucked into tight jeans that emphasized his long legs. A hand-tooled leather belt circled his narrow waist. Just like that, he had turned into the sexy rancher.

"Good morning," she said.

He turned to smile at her, moved a skillet and crossed the room to her. "Good morning," he said in a husky voice. "You look pretty." He hugged her lightly and paused to look into her eyes while his arm still circled her waist. Desire was obvious in his blue eyes and she needed to move away, but for an instant she was immobile, caught and held, wanting him to lean down and kiss her.

With an effort, she stepped away.

"I want to take Cody to look at the horses today and let him ride with me. Want to go with us?"

"Sure. I wouldn't miss Cody's first ride. I'll take pictures. Right now, he's still sleeping soundly."

"We're just hanging out at the ranch and I'm not joining the guys to do any work while we're here, so if you want to go into town or do something, let me know. This is a very quiet place."

"Frankly, a very quiet place sounds wonderful. Cody's going to have a great time. I know you'll look out for him and I'll be in charge of pictures. This will be special for him."

"It's special for me in a lot of ways," Nick said, touching a lock of her hair. "I forget how much I love it out here and I want both of you to like it, too. I've hardly been here in the past couple of years."

"You're too busy. Nick, you've got to slow down and smell the roses."

He smiled at her. "There are some other things I'd rather slow down to do," he said in a husky voice.

"And just what would you like to do?" she asked in a breathless voice, knowing she might as well toy with sticks of dynamite, but it had been aeons since she had flirted with anyone.

She caught the brief startled look as his eyes widened, and then Nick stepped closer. "Kiss you good morning," he said, taking her into his arms.

She had opened her mouth to say something, but words were lost when his mouth covered hers and he held her tightly to kiss her.

After the first startled moment, she wrapped her arms around him and kissed him in return, her heart pounding, knowing that she was going up in flames and encouraging him in every way. Guarding her heart had gone away days ago.

She finally ended the kiss and stepped away from him, fanning herself with her hand. "That starts the day with fireworks."

"That starts the day in one of the best possible ways."

She turned to find him watching her intently. "I'm not asking what the other possible ways are. I think I'll cool down with some orange juice."

"Coward," he said softly, but there was no bite in his words.

He walked back to get her a glass of juice. "I'll cook you an omelet. Tell me what you'd like."

"I can cook my own, Nick."

"I know you can, but I'll do it. Look at all the ingredients I have." She walked closer and saw little dishes of chopped mushrooms, onions, sweet peppers, jalapeño peppers, garlic, asparagus, basil leaves, spinach leaves. She looked up in surprise. "How early did you get up?"

"Early, but I can't take credit. Douglas had all this ready. He left it for us."

"Mercy, what a spread. Very tempting," she said, looking at the ingredients again and glancing at Nick to find him watching her with another intent look.

"What? Is something wrong?"

"Far, far from wrong," he said, his voice dropping lower, stirring more sizzles in her. "What's tempting in this kitchen isn't the chopped veggies."

Smiling, her heart beating faster, she moved away from him to sip her orange juice. "I'll have a bit of everything in my omelet. How's that? Can you cram it all in and still have a small omelet?"

"Just watch," he said, turning his attention to his cooking.

Was he flirting to see if he still held appeal or was he flirting for the fun of it? She wondered if she would always suspect his motives.

It was midmorning before they were on horseback. Claire took pictures of Cody, whose eyes sparkled. In his parka, Western hat, jeans and boots, he looked like a little cowboy and he sat on the big horse in front of Nick looking as if he had been given the world.

In addition to appearing almost as happy as his son, Nick was handsome, sexy and appealing in his black broad-brimmed hat, tight jeans that hugged his muscled legs and his boots. Would he kiss her again tonight? With the question came the realization that she wanted him to.

The more time she spent with him, the more she wanted to be with him and wanted to be in his arms, which was not going to help her in dealing with him.

"Well, you've cinched your place in his heart," she told Nick, looking up at him. "I imagine you can do no wrong in his eyes and there is no man on this earth who could possibly be a more wonderful dad."

"I hope you're right," Nick said. "That's awesome, but I love it. We can come out to the corral tonight after dinner when the guys spend a couple of hours riding and it'll be an eye-opener. I don't think he realizes what this animal can do. Has he ever been to a rodeo?"

She gave Nick a look.

"Well, we'll remedy that soon, maybe tomorrow night if I can find one somewhere we can get to."

"That will be the crowning touch."

Their busy schedules were not going to allow many more weeks like this one and the past weekend, when they had both cleared their calendars, so things would change soon. In the meantime, Claire was going to enjoy every moment.

All day she trailed after them, mostly to take pictures of Cody. And that night she sat down to another delicious meal with them, courtesy of Douglas and his wife who served them.

After dinner Claire passed on going to the corral to watch the cowboys with the horses.

When Nick and Cody returned, Cody ran to tell her about the bucking horses and the cowboys. He jabbered and waved his hands and she got out her iPad to take a video to show her grandmother. Cody didn't seem to notice the iPad. When he told her about his dad riding a bucking horse, she glanced at Nick in surprise. He grinned and she realized again that Nick loved ranch life, even the more rugged moments. If he hadn't been born a Milan with their legend and traditions, would his life and his choices have been different?

"Cody, I think it's time to call Grandma and go to bed so you'll be able to do things tomorrow."

"Yes, ma'am," he said as she got out her phone.

As he got ready for bed, Cody tugged on her wrist, and when she looked at him he continued telling her about the bucking horses. Nick joined them while she read to Cody and minutes after he climbed into bed he was asleep.

"Let's go look at the pictures you took today. I would like some copies." Nick draped his arm across her shoulders and they went to the sitting room to sit on the sofa together.

"I think you had another hit this evening. To say he was impressed is an understatement."

"I've told him he doesn't go around the horses unless I'm with him or Mr. Macklin, my foreman. Dusty Macklin has raised five boys and he knows kids. I would trust him with Cody, but nearly all the time Cody will be with me if he's on the ranch."

"I'm glad to hear that. You have a bull or two somewhere on the place, horses and rattlesnakes. Heaven knows what else, so I hope he's always with you."

"Don't ever worry about him here," Nick said, his blue eyes clear and direct. "Let's see the pics."

Together they went through the pictures, laughing over them. At one point Nick paused. "Claire, there's something I was thinking about even before this week. Christmas is coming. I know you have Christmas with your grandparents, and I don't want to interfere, but I want Cody around and my family will, too. Would you and Cody come back during Christmas week to have a Christmas together here at the ranch or in Dallas and include my parents? Your grandmother would be invited, and if I can possibly fly your grandfather here, he would be, too."

She hadn't wanted to think that Nick might want Cody with him at Christmastime, but now she had to make a decision. Once again her life was getting tied to Nick's and she felt on course for another giant hurt.

"If I can have Christmas morning at home with my grandparents, then we could come that afternoon, providing the weather is good enough to travel. If Grandpa can't travel, you can always join us in Houston. We'd be happy to have you."

"Thanks. I'll watch the weather. If it's good, I might have everyone here on the ranch. If not, we'll have Christmas in Dallas. We'll work it out however you agree, but that's great. What about putting a tree up while you're here? I don't want to do it all alone. We can cut a cedar here on the ranch and there are some decorations in the attic."

"Sure. Cody would love to decorate a tree," she said, wondering how much Nick was going to change her life.

"That's great. Thanks," he said, smiling.

She realized Nick was relaxed, happier and more light-hearted since they had arrived at the ranch. "It's so obvious how much you like it here, Nick. You ought to try to come more often."

"This ranch is my first love. Sometimes I envy Tony. But I can't do that to Dad. He's been good to me, helped me, and I have a good career and a good life because of him. A very good career, but I still love this life more."

"You're going to spend your life doing something you don't really love, just to please your father?"

"You've gone into a family business. Would you have chosen real estate if it hadn't been something you were raised to do?"

Taken aback by his question, she thought about her

answer as she looked into his blue eyes. "I thought about interior design, being a decorator. I like that. Even now, sometimes I can help a customer with staging a house before it's put on the market to sell."

"There, see? You're not so different."

"Not really. I don't have a whole different personality when I get involved with interior decorating. You do when you're on the ranch. You're far more laid-back and seem happier here. You're not attached to your cell phone out here."

"I turn it off. Right now it's in the kitchen." He shrugged. "I'll live here when I retire."

"Nick, you will have lived most of your life by then," she said.

"Worried about me?" he asked, his tone changing as he picked her up and placed her on his lap. Before she could answer, he kissed her and she was lost in his kisses then, wanting him more than she had before.

Need was more intense, and this time when his hands slipped beneath her knit shirt, she didn't want him to stop. Memories of making love with him bombarded her while longing spurred her to let go and love him.

Her fingers twisted free the buttons of his shirt and she ran her hands across his muscled chest, pushing away his shirt. Still kissing her, Nick shook off his shirt and tugged hers over her head to toss it away.

"Nick—" she started to protest, but his mouth covered hers and ended her words as he pulled her closer against his shoulder and kissed her passionately. Unfastening her bra, he slipped it off, his hands drifting lightly over her breasts. He caressed and teased, creating more need as she clung to him. A scarf held her hair behind her head. He unfastened it and combed his fingers through the long, luxurious strands.

Common sense cautioned her to stop. Each caress, each kiss complicated the situation and also moved her closer to another broken heart. But desire burned away caution.

Standing, he picked her up as he kissed her and carried her into his bedroom. He never broke contact, placing her down on her feet. She was so wrapped up in his lips on hers, his hands on her body, that she stopped worrying about their situation. More than even her next breath she wanted to just give herself over to the moment, over to Nick. She could no longer deny—to him or to herself—that she wanted him with an intensity that set her ablaze.

She let herself explore him, indulging for a moment the fantasies that had played out in her mind so many nights over the last four years. She ran her hands down his smooth back, slipping around his narrow waist to unbuckle his belt and tug it away. She could feel his erection pressing against her and wanted to free him, to get the barriers of clothing tossed aside.

Yet, at the same time, that niggling voice of reason echoed in her mind, telling her to stop and think about what she was doing. What kind of commitment was she about to make?

When Nick unfastened her jeans and his fingers moved beneath her clothing to caress and stroke her, she silenced that voice and let herself bask in the sensation, until she gasped with need and held him tightly.

He cupped one soft breast, his tongue swirling over and teasing the nipple. Clinging to his shoulders, she gasped with pleasure. He shifted one leg between hers, granting his hand more access to the source of pleasure between her thighs. His intimate strokes caused her to cry out again.

Just as she reached the point of no return, common sense slammed into her again and she stilled his hand. "Nick, we can't do this," she said. "There are so many reasons, not the least of which is I'm not protected." She looked up at him. Dark locks of his hair fell over his forehead. Tinged with desire, his blue eyes had darkened to the color of stormy seas. His mouth was red from their kisses. His male body was muscled, virile, perfect. She had to drag her eyes away.

"I've got protection," he said as he moved over her on the bed, still keeping all his weight from coming down on her. He held her as he showered kisses on her neck and throat. "I want you, Claire," he said between kisses. "I want you with all my being. You've given me back life and laughter and hope. The sex was always fantastic and that's real living."

"You have solutions and answers for everything. It's the politician in you." She didn't recognize her own voice; it was deep and husky with desire. She wanted him too, so badly it was nearly killing her to resist him. "But we are going to complicate our lives, Nick."

"We've already complicated the hell out of our lives." He pulled back to look at her, his lidded eyes irresistible. "Tell me you don't want this. Tell me when to stop." Even as he said those words, his one hand caressed her breast while the other hand stroked her inner thighs slowly, so lightly she ached to rise up and feel the full power of his touch.

She moaned, unable to dredge up the words to stop even though she knew she should. She wanted his mouth and hands on her. She wanted him inside her. She loved him and longed for him to make love to her again, all night long.

"I should tell you to stop," she whispered, her hand sliding over him, taking his thick rod in her hand to caress him.

"No, you shouldn't and you don't really want to," he murmured as he showered kisses on her breasts and drifted lower. His tongue trailed over her stomach, down between her thighs that she parted for him.

"Nick," she whispered, sitting up to kiss and stroke him, to try to build desire in him to the height he had in her. She wanted to kiss him from head to toe, to make love as she had longed to do so many times in so many empty nights. Now Nick was here in her arms and she was already beyond the point of stopping. This had been a dream of hers for years; now she was about to make it a reality. She pushed him down on the bed and caressed his hard body with her eyes before she followed with her hands, relishing the feel of him, wanting to build need in him until he wouldn't ever want to let her go. She was running headlong into heartbreak and disaster and she didn't care. She wanted him too desperately.

She moved over him, her hands fluttering, titillating him while she showered him with wet kisses. She trailed her tongue down his chest, and lower, lavishing kisses along his inner thighs. With a groan he grabbed her arms to roll her over, but she pushed him back down on the bed. "Wait, Nick. Just wait and let me love you."

She did, and the more she touched him, the more she wanted him. Memories taunted her, longing filled her, making her shake with need.

This time when he shifted she let him move her onto her back. He paused only long enough to look at her. "I want you," he whispered and then kissed away any answer she might have had.

He reached out to open a drawer and get a condom. She watched him, her gaze raking over his lean, muscled body, his strong shoulders and flat stomach. He was aroused, ready to love her. She wanted him and she was probably falling more in love with him than ever, something she'd feared would happen this week.

As he moved over her again, she opened wide for him, wanting him, thinking of all the nights she had dreamed of this moment when she hadn't thought it would ever happen again.

He entered her slowly, filling her, hot and hard, and she stopped thinking then, just moving, wanting him and crying out with need. He began to move slowly, driving her wild with wanting him, tension coiling tightly in her.

She clung to him, relishing that it was Nick in her arms, the man she loved and the man whose love she wanted in return. She ran her hands over his back, down over his buttocks, as they moved in perfect synchrony.

Passion swept her up, higher and higher, until she reached the apex of her desire, and with a throaty gasp leaped into ecstasy. Only then did she feel Nick lose his iron control. He pumped wildly as she kept with him. Release burst over her, shattering her, in a climax unlike any other.

His weight came down and he held her, turning his head as he kissed her cheek. They both gasped for breath while he held her close.

"You've given me so much, Claire," he whispered.

She combed locks of his hair back from his damp forehead.

He was quiet, just holding her close, and she held him, remaining just as silent, deep in her thoughts. After a while he rolled onto his side but he continued to hold her close. "I want you with me all night," he said.

"I can't do that, Nick." It pained her, but she couldn't stay the night in his bed. "I'll go in a while."

"You're a tough woman sometimes," he whispered, caressing her cheek.

"So, you think I've been tough the past hour?" she teased.

His arm circled her waist and he pulled her closer even

though he was almost covering her with his body. "Not tough. Sexy beyond my wildest dreams." His eyes darkened again and she wondered if he was feeling desire again so soon. "I admire you, Claire. You know what you want and you stick to it." He gave her a quick grin. "But you do know there's such a thing as compromise?"

"Compromise is for politicians. I have to do what I think is best for Cody, for me and for my family. Maybe I made the wrong choices by not telling you about my pregnancy and not telling you about his birth, but I thought I was doing what was best for all of us—Cody, me and my family. Actually, after a certain point, I thought it was what was best for you, too."

"Stop worrying about all that. It's done and over. Let me just hold you close."

They were quiet again as he held her and stroked her back. "This is good, Claire."

She didn't answer him, certain they hadn't made anything easier tonight.

"I don't want to let you go," he said.

"You'll have to soon," she answered, even though she wished he'd never let her go. But there was no way with their circumstances.

Finally she rolled away, starting to get up, but Nick's arm tightened around her waist and he drew her back. "Don't go."

"Nick, I'm not staying here all night."

He released her and she stepped out of bed. He lay there and watched her as she gathered her clothes. "Good night, Claire," he said before she reached the door.

She turned to look at him. He sat back in his big bed with his hands propped behind his head and a sheet across his lap. Her mouth went dry and she wanted to be back in his arms, to stay the rest of the night with him.

Tonight hadn't brought them any closer to a solution, but had simply complicated her life and made Nick far more difficult to resist. She wouldn't make it any worse by giving into the temptation and staying with him. Steeling herself, she turned away and hurried to her room.

Thursday morning after breakfast, Nick had a pickup parked at the back gate. It was a blustery day with wind gusts that carried a winter chill, and after breakfast, when Nick announced they would go select a tree, she gave Cody his parka and gloves. She pulled on her heavy coat, turning the fur collar up to protect her neck.

"You need some boots out here, Claire."

"I have socks and sneakers," she said, watching him pull on a warm shearling-lined leather jacket. He had black leather gloves and his broad-brimmed black Stetson, which made him look just as good with his clothes on as he had naked last night. She stopped that thought before it made her hot and uncomfortable in her coat. She was grateful that Cody was almost dancing with excitement beside her and needed her attention. She helped him put on his little gloves.

Nick carried Cody to the truck. Gusts of wind whipped against them as they climbed into the warm truck with the motor already running.

They drove to an isolated area that held a scattering of tall cedars.

Nick and Cody selected a tree while she took more pictures. She watched Nick work to chop down the tree, her gaze drifting across his broad shoulders and strong back as he wielded the heavy ax. Nick looked as happy as Cody and she thought he missed a lot of this ranch life locked into working so hard at a career that wasn't his first love.

It wasn't for the money; she knew that much about him. He had to be doing it to please his dad.

A light snow began to fall, sending Cody into gales of excitement as he danced around. "It's snowing," he cried, waving his arms and catching flakes.

"Doesn't take much to please him, does it?" Nick remarked, laughing.

"Everything out here dazzles him and this snow is just one more added touch. We don't see much snow in Houston. You know, he may love the ranch even more than his dad."

Nick looked startled, turning to her and then looking at Cody with a slight frown, and she wondered what he was thinking. He turned to finish his task of chopping down the big cedar. As soon as he'd loaded the felled tree into the truck, they headed home.

By the time they reached the back door and Nick hauled the tree inside, a blizzard was raging. Cody was torn between watching Nick set up the tree and rubbing circles in the frosty glass to look at the snow.

After dinner Nick brought boxes of ornaments from his attic. "Next year we'll get ornaments in Verity or Dallas or Houston, so we have our own. These are some from Mom that I grew up with and some that I bought in haste and then never even opened because I had to go back to Dallas. The ones Karen and I had are in the attic in Dallas," he said. Then he added, "I thought you'd wonder about them."

"It doesn't matter. They're all new to Cody," she said. "I'll let you take the lead with decorating and I'll continue to take more pictures."

Nick smiled as he opened a box. "Cody, let me get the lights strung on first and then you can start decorating."

Claire helped Nick with the lights, brushing against him, aware of him moving close beside her, once looking into his eyes to see his expression change. For a moment she was lost in his gaze, seeing desire flare in the depths of blue. Her heart skipped and she remembered last night in his arms. Taking a deep breath, she turned away.

Finally, they had the tree done, the top portion sparsely decorated and most ornaments on the lower half where Cody could reach.

Nick turned off all but the tree lights. On the other side of the tree, through the window, they could see the blowing snow still falling, the ground now covered. They all stood back to look at the tree, Nick in the middle with his arms around Cody and her. "That is a splendid Christmas tree," Nick said.

She was aware of Nick's arm across her shoulders as she stood pressed against his side. Cody reached over to slip his small hand into hers and she looked at her son, who looked dazzled and happy with a huge smile on his face as he stared at the tree.

A pang tore at her heart. They weren't a family and it hurt. She glanced up at Nick to find him looking down at her with a somber expression and she wondered what he was thinking. Did he realize what obstacles they faced?

"It's the best Christmas tree," Cody said in his child's voice, which caused another ache in her heart.

"I think it's beautiful," she remarked, thinking it was and knowing she would always remember this night and this moment, holding her son's hand and standing in the circle of Nick's arm. It was all a reminder of what she was lacking—a family of her own, a loving husband.

"It's a real tree that you cut down," Cody said in awe. "I like it best," he added, and she felt a twist to her heart. She would have to always share Cody at Christmas now with Nick. She was thankful that Nick would be a wonderful father for their son, but there were going to be some tough moments ahead, when Cody would have times in his life to do things with his dad and she would be no part of them.

Trying to avoid thinking about the rough moments, she moved away.

"Cody, it's way past your bedtime. Let's get you ready and then your dad can read his books to you." In the attic, when he'd gone to get the ornaments, Nick had found two old Christmas books he'd had as a child. He wanted to share them with Cody.

As Cody nodded, Nick swung him up on his shoulders and carried him from the room. She looked at them both and knew that, despite all the walls of defense that she'd erected, she was sinking more in love than ever with Nick.

Getting her iPad, Claire sent all the latest pictures to Nick, thinking about last night and wondering whether he expected a repeat tonight. Soon they would be back in Dallas, and then they'd go home on Sunday, and she felt her heart clutch.

She realized she had put herself at risk again by falling for someone who could easily walk out of her life as he had before.

How was she going to be able to work out shuffling Cody back and forth to DC? She ran her hand over her forehead, knowing problems loomed and they hadn't come one bit closer to a solution.

She looked down at the iPad at a picture of Nick and Cody on horseback. A handsome dad and an adorable son. She didn't dare give her thoughts to any "what-ifs."

She put down the iPad and went to her son's temporary room. Nick was turning out the light after having read the stories, and Cody was asleep, the covers tucked up under his chin.

When he entered the hall, Nick took her hand. "Come

here, Claire," he said, heading toward his room. As soon as they entered his sitting room, he closed the door.

"I've been waiting for this moment since last night," he said, wrapping his arms around her and leaning down to kiss her.

Warmth filled her as she wrapped her arms around him to kiss him in return. Even though she knew the folly of kissing him, she wanted to love him until he never wanted to let her go.

Ten

In the throes of an erotic dream, she realized she was getting poked in the arm by a small finger.

She opened her eyes to look at Cody. "Get up, Mama. It's morning. Dad said it's time for everyone to get up."

Smiling, she hugged Cody. "I'll get up and have a little talk with your dad. And where is your dad?"

"In the kitchen cooking. He said I could wake you, that you're a sleepyhead."

"Is that so? I'll be right there. You can go eat your breakfast while I get dressed."

As he ran out of the room, she got up to close the door. She realized then it was no erotic dream she'd been having. Instead she'd been reliving last night with Nick. Her thighs still throbbed deliciously from a night of lovemaking. They'd made love, showered together, and made love again, twice, before she'd come to her room. Sated and well loved, she'd slept like a baby.

Knowing her son awaited her, she showered and dressed

in jeans and a long-sleeved red T-shirt, and hurried to the kitchen.

"Miss Sleepyhead has arrived," she said, walking into the kitchen. Dressed in a black T-shirt and jeans, Nick was seated at the table across from Cody. Nick came to his feet when she entered and smiled at her as his gaze raked over her, sending fiery currents in its wake.

"I can think of a lot of other names that would be more appropriate," he said.

"You better not say them now," she threatened, smiling at him. "Thanks for feeding Cody."

"I'm getting the hang of it."

"Dad said we're going to build a snowman if the snow is wet enough. We'll go out after breakfast."

"And you are more than welcome to join us," Nick told her.

"Maybe for about ten minutes to take pictures." She laughed. "I'm going home with five thousand more pictures."

As Nick smiled, his gaze skimmed over her and her breath caught at the look in his eyes. She felt as if his fingers had drifted over her instead of just his eyes. She was susceptible to every glance, every touch from him, too aware of him. This had to stop or she'd never make it through the day.

"My images are in here," he said, tapping his head, his voice dropping a notch.

She knew what images he was referring to. Ones that would never be shared on Instagram. "And they better stay there and we hear no more about them," she said, and he grinned.

"This morning, with your permission, I'd like to take Cody out with me and let him see the men working. They'll break ice on the ponds and tanks so the animals can drink and put out hay for them. We'll be in the truck. I'll take good care of him."

"Do you want to go?" she asked Cody, knowing what he would answer.

"Yes, ma'am," he said, looking at Nick.

"Fine. I'll definitely pass on that one, though."

"I figured you would."

After breakfast she had fun with Nick and Cody as they made a snowman, and then she watched them as they left to go out onto the ranch. A tall cowboy holding the hand of his small son. When they returned she heard about their day in great detail and Nick showed her pictures of Cody he'd taken with his phone. Her son looked ecstatic out there with the cowboys.

After dinner that night Nick played games with Cody, lying on the floor with him and letting his son climb on him. She watched them and wondered whether Nick seemed so happy and relaxed because they were at the ranch or because he had Cody with him. Either way, his appeal heightened. There was no denying it. He was a marvelous dad for Cody.

But what kind of man was he for her?

She wanted to love someone who returned that love. What Nick felt for her was lust. He was sexy, virile, filled with energy, and he desired her and lusted after her, but he wasn't in love with her. He could walk away tomorrow, run for the US Senate, live in DC and seldom see her without it tearing him up.

He would miss her for sex, certainly, and maybe for how she could be at his side to help him in his career.

Not that that was going to happen, she told herself. Her grandfather was going through physical therapy in hopes he could return in a limited capacity to his office. She didn't want to get someone to run it and walk away, marry Nick and abandon the business and her grandparents.

Nick's deep laugh broke into her thoughts. Once more

she remarked on how much more she had heard Nick laugh, whistle and hum since he had been on the ranch. She wondered why he pursued the life he did if he was so much happier being a cowboy. Nick rolled away, stretched out a long arm and his hand closed around her ankle lightly, startling her and getting her attention.

"Why so solemn?" he asked as his fingers lightly caressed her ankle.

"I was wondering how I'm going to get him quiet enough to ever go to bed."

"I'll take care of him. Don't give it another thought." He rolled away and sat up. "Cody, it's bath time and then story time. Come get on my shoulders and I'll carry you."

Cody laughed and got on Nick's shoulders, winding his fingers in Nick's thick hair. Nick stood, smiled at her and trotted off like a horse, making Cody laugh harder.

She glanced at the clock. She would give them thirty minutes and then go kiss Cody good-night.

When she walked into the bedroom later, Nick was leaning down to brush Cody's forehead with a kiss. He crossed the room to place his arm around her shoulders.

"He couldn't last to hear the end of the story."

"Good job, Dad. Thank you very much," she said, aware of Nick close at her side. She felt his fingers toying with her hair.

In the hall he turned toward his room and stopped. "I have plans for us."

"I'm sure you do," she said, amused, but her smile vanished as she looked up at him. Desire was blatant in his blue eyes. He ran his hands lightly across her shoulders, up to caress her nape, to untie the ribbon that held her hair. He leaned down to brush her lips lightly with his.

He stroked her mouth with another kiss and then his

mouth covered hers and his tongue touched hers. As he kissed her, his arm tightened around her.

Breathless, she wanted him in return. Wrapping her arms around his neck, she pressed against him and kissed him back with fervor.

Nick picked her up and she knew without looking that he carried her to his suite. She heard the door close behind him and in seconds he'd laid her on the bed and joined her.

It was eight the next morning when she woke in her own room, then showered and dressed to go get breakfast and see where Cody and Nick were.

The family dinner was tonight, at Nick's house in Dallas. Briefly she felt butterflies at the thought and then remembered how friendly Wyatt had been and how super friendly Nick's parents had been. They made it obvious how badly they wanted Cody in the family and the butterflies left her. She joined Nick and Cody at the breakfast table, where they were eating bowls of oatmeal and berries.

"The temperature should climb today and the roads are clear," Nick said. "We're off to Dallas after breakfast and tonight should be fun. I can't wait for my family to get to know Cody."

"The only grandson—he should be very welcome," she said, smiling but feeling a pang in her heart. She would spend time with his family, but she'd never be a part of it.

By late morning they were back in Dallas at Nick's mansion. Two members of his staff were present and his cook was already there.

Cody sat at a game table in the family room, coloring, and Nick took her arm to pull her aside, walking into the hall.

"My folks will be here tonight. Can you talk to Cody— and I think it should be you—about what he would like to

call them? Granddad, Grandma—whatever he comes up
with will be wonderful to them. They'll be thrilled and
it would be nice to start now. They are his grandparents,
after all."

"Of course. I should have thought of that. I'll ask him
and then we'll get your approval."

"I think I can give approval right now," he said, smiling at her and brushing her cheek with a kiss. He looked
into her eyes and the moment changed. He pulled her to
him, to wrap his arms around her and really kiss her until
she made him stop.

"Whoa, Nick. Your house has staff and Cody's running
around. The hall isn't private."

"My bedroom will be tonight, and I can't wait."

"You'll have to," she said. "I'm going to talk to Cody,"
she added and left him. She had stopped him, but her heart
still raced and she couldn't stop that as easily.

Luckily the rest of the afternoon was taken up with
party preparations, so she was too busy to get waylaid by
tempting kisses.

Late in the afternoon Nick offered to get Cody ready
for the party, so she handed over his clothes and left the
two of them while she went to dress. It was a dinner party,
and the first time she would meet some of his family—and
she barely knew his parents. She'd chosen to wear a deep
scarlet, long-sleeved dress with a round neck and matching high-heeled pumps.

Brushing her hair, she let it fall around her face. She
fastened both the necklace from Nick and the bracelet,
looking at the charm of the man and the woman holding a
child's hands. She shook her head. That would not be her
with Cody and Nick. She suspected when she went home
this time, other than Christmas, she would see little of Nick

except to work out arrangements for Cody, something she dreaded more each day.

When she walked into the family room and Nick's gaze flashed over her, she saw the approval in his eyes. "You look great."

She turned to her son first. "Cody, you look very nice," she said, her gaze going over his blue sweater and navy slacks. The gold Junior Sheriff badge was pinned to his sweater.

"And so do you, Dad," she said, taking in his navy sport jacket over a long-sleeved pale blue shirt and navy slacks. He would be the best-looking Milan in the room.

Promptly at six the doorbell rang, and in minutes Nick's parents entered. They had another gift in their hands and she was certain it was for Cody.

He dutifully shook hands with Peter again and let Evelyn hug him. "Cody, we brought you a present," she said, as her husband held out the box.

"Thank you," he answered politely, glancing at Claire and she nodded.

"Open your present, Cody."

He tore off the paper and opened the box to pull out a stuffed hippo. Grinning, Cody clutched the hippo in his arms. "Thank you, Grandmother," he said and turned to Judge Milan. "Thank you, Granddad."

"You're very welcome," Peter said, smiling broadly. Judge Milan sat on a chair and leaned forward toward Cody. "Cody, we're so happy to have you call us Granddad and Grandmother. That's very, very nice."

"Yes, sir."

"You have raised the sweetest little boy who is so well-mannered," Evelyn said. She dabbed at her eyes, which surprised Claire. "I love him already and thank you for any time you share him with us. He's a wonderful child."

"Thank you. And thank you for the hippo for him. He'll love it."

The doorbell rang and in minutes Jake and Madison Calhoun entered. Nick crossed the room, taking Cody with him. "Claire, this is my sister Madison and her husband, Jake Calhoun. Meet Claire and my son, Cody," Nick said.

"We've met at an art gallery in Houston and it's nice to see you again, Claire," Madison said. "And you, too, Cody. What do you have in your arms?"

"My hippo. My grandmother and my granddad gave it to me."

"Referring to Mom and Dad," Nick said.

"I figured that much," Madison said, laughing. "Mom is beside herself with joy about Cody," she said. "I can see why. Nick, your son looks exactly like you."

"I think so," Nick said smiling. "Here come Wyatt and Destiny."

Wyatt greeted Claire with a big smile. "I hope you had a good time at the ranch."

"Cody has never had so much fun."

In short order she met Wyatt's wife, Destiny, a beautiful woman in a dramatic black dress with red trim. Then Nick's younger brother, Tony crouched down to talk to Cody. He took his nephew's hand after a moment and they walked away with Tony talking to him.

"He's a Pied Piper with kids and animals," Nick said. "Maybe he gets on their level, I don't know. He's single and he doesn't know beans about kids, but they love him."

She smiled, watching Cody with Tony as Cody laughed.

In a short time she began to feel she knew Nick's family better. She realized he had good relationships with his siblings and they saw each other fairly often. She also saw he was very close to his dad, who could be charming. Nick, in his way, was as close to his family as she was to hers.

He had never had to take care of any of his, or be responsible for them, so he saw that differently.

Everyone was interested in Cody, who seemed to be having a good time with all the adult attention.

With Douglas serving, they ate in Nick's spacious dining room. During dinner, Jake clinked his glass for quiet and everyone became silent as Madison spoke. "I want to take this time to make one announcement that I hope does not in any way detract from the joy of meeting Claire and Cody—Jake and I are expecting. I'm due next July."

Everyone clapped and cheered as she sat down and then dinner continued. Again, Claire couldn't keep from comparing how the Milan family was enthused over the expected baby and how there had not been a word from any of them during her pregnancy. Basically, it had been her fault for not telling Nick about the baby, but if they had known, at that time there would not have been applause and cheers. She glanced at Nick and was surprised to see him looking at her. She wondered if he shared her thoughts.

The party was fun because Nick's siblings enjoyed each other. Once during the evening she looked over to see Cody sitting in Judge Milan's lap as the judge showed Cody a trick. The impact wasn't lost on her. Changes were already taking place in her life, she realized. But at the same time she was pleased that his grandparents liked her son and glad he liked them, as well.

When Nick's parents left at nine, Evelyn hugged Claire. "Thank you for telling us we can come visit Cody in Houston."

"I meant what I said. We'd love to have you, and you're more than welcome to stay at my house. I have a big home and that would make Cody happy."

"That is so sweet, Claire. We'll take you up on the offer soon."

As his mother headed toward the door, Claire looked beyond her to see Nick watching her with a solemn expression. As she closed the door behind his parents, Nick stepped close. "So, they get to visit and stay at your house and I don't."

"It isn't quite the same, but you can stay. I may not be there, but Grandma will be happy to have you."

"That isn't quite the same, either," he said. After a moment he shook his head. "Anyway, thanks for being so gracious to my parents."

"They're my son's grandparents and I think he's going to love them," she said, turning to walk away. She let Cody stay up until ten, but then she put him to bed and rejoined the others.

By the time the last couple left it was almost midnight. As Nick watched them drive away, he draped his arm across her shoulders. "Everyone loved Cody and each one was happy to see you. It was a great night. Now, let's go in. Finally I get to be alone with you," he said, closing the door and heading to his suite. "Claire, you were wonderful tonight and so was Cody. Both of you charmed my family. My parents are shocking in their reaction to Cody, because I never expected them to be this way. You know, when I mentioned to them that when I live in Austin they won't see Cody, they both looked unhappy."

Surprised, she stared at Nick. "Your dad, too?"

"Even my dad," he replied with a nod of his head. "The other thing is, I hadn't really noticed age changing them until tonight. Dad is more mellow, less energetic, but he's changed, and now with Cody I think they're both changing more."

Continuing to stare at Nick, she wondered how much their reactions would influence Nick. "Nick, if your dad is unhappy about you living in Austin when the legislature is in session, that's a huge change."

"You and Cody have turned my world, and maybe theirs, upside down. Upside down for the good," Nick said, looking intently at her. Her heart missed a beat. Was there any chance of Nick changing his political ambitions? Had the time spent at the ranch with Cody caused him to look at his life differently? A bigger question loomed in her mind. Was there a chance of Nick falling in love?

Before she could pursue a response, Nick closed the door to his suite and turned to her. "Now, let's forget family, the evening, everything except you and me. I've been waiting all day for this moment," he said, leaning down to kiss her. Held in his crushing embrace, she forgot everything else except Nick as she returned his kisses.

Long after Nick had fallen asleep, she remained awake, thinking about this past week and their future. She was in love with Nick, and his thoughtfulness, his growing love for Cody, his lovemaking, everything between them was making that love stronger and she couldn't deal with another hurt that would be bigger than when they had parted before he married.

She had to put distance between them or risk a giant hurt—a hurt that would involve Cody this time.

She needed to distance herself from Nick. Lust was not the same as love and there was no future in it.

Nick had his future mapped out, and it did not include marriage to her any more now than it had four years ago.

As difficult as it was going to be, she had to stop what was superficial and meaningless between them because she couldn't be intimate with Nick without losing her heart, but he could easily be enveloped in lust and not have his heart involved.

Tears burned her eyes and rolled down her cheeks. She

wiped them away and tried to get a grip on her emotions. She already loved him and she already hurt, but it could get worse and maybe she could save herself a bigger hurt. She should put an end to seeing him every time Cody did.

It was four in the morning when she pulled on a robe and faced Nick as she stood beside the bed. "I'm going to my room. You think about how we can work out sharing Cody. Your family will want to know him and you'll want time with him. You come up with a plan and we'll go from there."

Nick pulled the sheet around his waist and got up, walking around the bed to place his hands on her shoulders. She stood looking up at him, trying to focus while she was aware of his bare, muscled chest, his broad shoulders, only the sheet low on his hips as they faced each other. She had to resist him, but it was growing more difficult by the day.

"I'll do that. I'm not in a rush and I know it will take time to work things out. He's too little to come see me without you unless I come get him."

She shook her head. "I'm not coming to see you along with him, and I don't think you'd want that either. You think about what you want. This can't keep on. My emotions get caught up in intimacy, so in a way, this is goodbye between us. I'll still see you with Cody and family around, but that's all, Nick. Your life is set and so is mine and they don't fit together. We have to stop before we both get hurt badly again."

"What you're saying makes sense, but I don't want to say goodbye, Claire."

"We don't have a future—you and I—and I'm not going to continue to sleep with you occasionally when we're together. I get my emotions entangled. This is a private goodbye to intimacy, to moments alone or dinners out or dates. We'll just get hurt again otherwise." She turned and walked away to go to her own room.

Sunday after Nick put them on the plane he waved as it taxied away. Claire and Cody were at the window and both waved. He hated to see them go, feeling as if part of his heart was being ripped away. It startled him how empty he felt with Claire and Cody gone. He had learned to live alone the past two years, but now life loomed like one big void and he wanted Claire with him. Her goodbye had hurt. The thought of her going out of his life again—except for brief moments—seemed unbearable. The realization startled him. How deep did his feelings for her run?

As he drove home, he thought about his parents and their plans to visit Claire in Houston. They'd never been interested in getting to know her before. He thought, too, about their unhappy looks when he mentioned living in Austin. For the first time, Nick wondered if his dad would rather he didn't pursue a political career.

Claire's question echoed in his mind. Had he pursued politics for himself or for his dad?

Nick watched the road and turned into the drive, stopping before going through the gates. He felt as if his life had been built on shifting sand and he wasn't certain where he stood any longer. How deep were his feelings for Claire? Had he been consumed by lust or did he really want her as a part of his life outside his bedroom?

He didn't know the answers. He only knew he'd better figure it out soon.

As soon as he arrived home, he got out his cell phone to catch up on all the calls he had missed and pour himself into work. He tried to get back into his regular routine, but he couldn't keep his mind on work and he finally shoved it aside to think about how they would share Cody.

DC wouldn't come up for several years, but he would be in Austin most of the time from January until June, when his term was over. He thought about Claire's family and the care she continued to give them, plus the company she ran now with three offices in the Houston area. He sat thinking about her ties and his own, comparing them, and in minutes he was lost, remembering this past week on the ranch and the fun they'd had, the joy he'd felt watching Cody.

Maybe it was just because he had told Claire and Cody goodbye this morning that he was unhappy and missed them so much.

He thought Monday would be better, when he was back at work and busy.

But as he dressed for work the next morning, he was lost again in memories of Claire. Nick missed her. He walked to his bedroom to stare at his bed and remembered Claire in his arms. How right and good it had felt. He couldn't fathom not making love to her again. He missed her each time he had said goodbye to her, but the past two times, before she came to the ranch, he knew he would be with her again within days. Now he faced a future in which he would just see her briefly as he picked up Cody or took him home. And maybe not even then. He might just see her grandmother or the nanny.

What were his feelings for her now?

Life had been great on the ranch with Claire and Cody there. Now he felt empty without her, hopeless, hurt beyond words. He'd tried to guard his heart against falling for Claire, even telling himself it was impossible to fall in love with her a second time. He'd let himself have fun with her, allowed himself to bed her, thinking his heart had been secure.

But he'd been wrong.

To hurt this badly over her goodbye, he realized, he

had to be in love with her. And he might be losing the best possible life and the best possible woman for reasons that wouldn't ever bring him real happiness.

He was in love, and he'd better do something about it.

He pulled out his phone to call her, but when he heard a recorded message he put away his phone. "Claire." He whispered her name, wanting her, missing her and wishing he could conjure her up before him. He didn't want to lose her this time. But how could they work out getting together now when they couldn't do it four years ago?

Would Claire yield on any part of her life to try to be together, or did she even care? What could he change to make her happy? There had to be a way to work things out, but this time he'd better be certain about what he really wanted in life and what he could give up.

Would a political career be worth losing her? Even if he wanted to be a rancher, the only way to get Claire in his life was to move to Houston.

Was there any way to move Claire and keep her happy about the move? He crossed to his desk to make a list of all the things in Houston that were important to her. He stared blankly at the paper, sorting through all kinds of possibilities. There had to be a way...

Monday, Claire called in to say she would be late to the office. She didn't feel like concentrating on work. She missed Nick, and it surprised her how much. She missed his flirting and his companionship, and she missed the hours of passion. She loved him more than she had when she was younger. She had thought she was over the heartbreak when he came back into her life. Instead, she was more drawn to him than ever, while it was less likely they could ever get together as a couple. Yet she would have to see him because of their son.

She was going to have to discuss sharing Cody, but she'd told Nick to get a plan. He was the one who wanted changes, so he could come up with something and she would have to try to work with him.

She could not leave Houston or her family obligations, which were now greater than ever. She would not abandon her grandparents or shut down the agency that meant so much to her grandfather and that they had both worked so hard to build.

One thing had changed, though—Nick's parents. She had seen the looks on their faces when he had mentioned they would not see Cody when he was in Austin. If they didn't see Cody when Nick was in Austin, they definitely would not if Nick lived in DC, and his parents were smart enough to realize that.

She never guessed his parents would care about Cody because they hadn't even bothered to try to meet her when their son had hoped to marry her. It had been a shock to find out how badly they wanted a grandchild and how much they loved Cody from the first moment. When they asked if they could visit, she had agreed and meant it. That was a giant change—would it have any influence on Nick and his decisions?

Her thoughts turned to Nick again and the wonderful week with him on the ranch that had been paradise. She missed him and it had taken all her willpower not to answer his call moments ago. She loved him and she missed him. She couldn't see any way to work out a future sharing Cody with him, but she had to.

She was alone in her room and she gave in to tears, for just a moment letting go and hurting, wondering how she would cope with seeing Nick only for minutes at a time. Or worse, watching him once again marry someone else.

It was going to hurt watching him take Cody for days

at a time, but she would never deny him that right or hurt her son. He was good for Cody, a wonderful dad, and Cody already loved him. In a lot of ways she was thankful that Nick was in Cody's life, filling a void that needed to be filled. Too bad he could never be part of *her* life.

She heard her phone and saw that it was Nick again. She didn't take the call. She couldn't talk to him yet. She didn't want to burst into tears while they were on the phone. In minutes she received a brief text: Have a plan to discuss about Cody. Can you go to dinner next Thursday and we'll talk about it? I can pick you up at 7. Would like to come at 6 so I can see Cody.

She typed her reply. She would go, wondering what Nick had in mind and if the evening would dissolve in sharp words the way it had so long ago, the night he had proposed.

Later that morning her grandmother left, taking Cody for a haircut and errands. As Claire nibbled at a late breakfast, the doorbell rang. She answered to find a deliveryman on her porch holding a giant arrangement of red roses, white orchids, red anthurium and white gladioli. A box wrapped in blue paper and tied with a big blue bow was delivered with the flowers.

As soon as she closed the door, she removed a card from the flowers that read: *To Claire: Thank you for the joy you have brought us with our grandson. Love, Peter and Evelyn.*

Startled, she looked at the flowers again. She would never know, but she wondered…if she had told Nick about her pregnancy, would things have worked out differently? It was a question that couldn't be answered. Back then, even though it was only four years ago, Nick's dad was still deeply intent on having his son move up in politics. It was obvious, now that Cody was here and the Milans were older, that that wasn't what the judge wanted for his son. He wanted his grandson in his life and in Evelyn's.

Claire removed a card from the box and saw it was to Cody from them. She smiled. Cody had four doting grandparents now. If only she and Nick—

Claire stopped instantly. She was not going to live on wishes. She would have to pick up and go on, work out something with Nick and try to live with it. She'd have to live with the hurt.

She was still telling herself that on Thursday as she dressed for the evening with Nick.

Cody stayed downstairs, playing in the family room while her grandmother was nearby. Claire was running a few minutes late, and when she heard the door chimes, she knew Cody and Grandma would both enjoy talking to Nick.

When Claire was finally ready, she assessed her image in the mirror. She smoothed her navy long-sleeved dress with a straight skirt and fingered the diamond pendant and charm bracelet. Then she picked up her small black purse and went downstairs, hoping against hope that she had her emotions under control.

Nick heard Claire seconds before she walked into the room. He stood immediately while his heart thudded. She looked stunning. He felt hot, dazzled and had to make an effort to avoid staring at her. He longed to cross the room to take her into his arms.

She smiled, her full, red lips curving and tugging on his senses. He wanted to be alone with her, back in his suite where nothing could disturb them.

"Have a seat, Nick. I'm sure Grandma and Cody are enjoying talking to you."

"Nick said he got a present for me, but the last time

he was here, I was gone, so he brought it tonight," Verna said, holding out a box. Claire crossed the room to look at a beautiful gold locket on a thin golden chain with her grandmother's initials carved into the face of the locket. She opened it and inside the locket were two pictures, one of Claire and Cody and another of Cody.

"Nick, that's lovely," Claire said, smiling at him and then looking at her grandmother. "I know you'll love it. Turn around and I'll put it on you," she said.

Her grandmother shifted in her chair and Claire fastened the locket around her neck. Verna turned back around and looked down at it. "That's beautiful, Nick. I'll treasure it. Thank you."

"I'm glad you like it."

"I got a present, too," Cody said, holding out a book.

Claire took it in her hands. "Great, Cody. Another new book, and I'll bet you and Grandma can read it at bedtime," she said, smiling at Nick.

Cody looked at his grandmother who nodded. "Of course, we will," she said.

They spent the next thirty minutes talking until Claire stood. "I'm guessing Nick has some dinner reservations somewhere."

Nick came to his feet and picked up Cody. "Be a good kid tonight and I'll see you in the morning."

Cody hugged him and kissed Nick's cheek. "Thank you for the book."

"You're very welcome. We'll read it in the morning." Nick hugged him and kissed his cheek. He carried him to the door to hug him one more time before setting him down.

Nick escorted Claire to the passenger side of his car, then got in and drove out of her neighborhood.

"You look gorgeous. I didn't tell you back there, but

that's what I was thinking," he said, keeping his attention on the road, but remembering clearly the impact she'd had when she stepped into the doorway. She had always dazzled him, from the first moment at the cocktail party where he met her, but she seemed to have more of an effect on him now that she was several years older.

"Thank you," she said. "You look very handsome yourself. I suspect you'll win most of the female votes the next time you run."

He smiled. "I hope my looks aren't the basis of votes," he said.

Nick drove to a tall hotel with sparkling Christmas lights strung over the wide entrance. He stopped in the drive to let the engine idle while he turned to her. "This is my hotel. How about dinner in my room where we can be free to talk about possibilities and what we can do to share Cody? I don't want to be in a restaurant. This could get emotional, Claire."

She had to agree, but reluctance filled her because her life was going to change again.

Eleven

Claire's heart beat faster as she nodded. "As long as it's just dinner and conversation, Nick. Nothing else. I can't keep…" She couldn't bring herself to say the words *making love*, not when they conjured hot images of a naked Nick. "I just want to hear your suggestions, see what we can work out for Cody and then go home."

"I've ordered dinner from a restaurant and they should have it in about half an hour. I got lobster for you, steak for me—how's that?"

"Excellent choices," she said, wondering if tonight would be another heartbreak. She was going to have to share Cody with Nick and she dreaded what he might propose.

Driving to the door, Nick gave the valet his keys and took Claire's arm to enter the hotel and take an elevator to his suite on the top floor. "I got you a little Christmas present," he said, unlocking the door. Barely aware of her elegant surroundings as Nick took her coat and slipped his off, she saw a small rosemary plant decorated as a Christmas tree in the center of a glass table by the sofa. One present was tucked into the branches, a small box wrapped in shiny red paper and tied with silver ribbon.

"The Christmas tree is mine, not the hotel's. The present is for you, but before you open it, let's talk," he said while she looked into his thickly lashed blue eyes, which could make her heartbeat quicken with just a glance. Her gaze drifted to his mouth and she drew a deep breath. Could she get through this evening without succumbing to his kisses? Or without getting emotional and crying?

He cleared his throat before he began, and for a moment she thought he looked nervous. "First, I've had time to think about us. The week with you and Cody at the ranch was special." He stepped closer to place his hands on her waist. She could have sworn he was trembling. Then he said the words she thought she'd never hear him speak again. The words she dreaded now.

"Claire, I love you."

She closed her eyes and took a deep breath, hurt rippling inside. "Even though I've tried to get over you, I think I've always loved you," she said, opening her eyes and looking up at him. "But that just compounds the problems between us without solving any of them."

But Nick wouldn't be stopped. "I want to be with you and Cody. I want to share my life with you," he said.

She frowned. He knew all the impossible obstacles. Surely this wasn't going to be a second round of the fight they'd had when they split four years earlier.

"You've made me stop and think, Claire. That week on the ranch was the best week of my life. Maybe I'm missing really living, having love and a family in my life. I've thought about what you want and need, and what I want and need—what I can give up to make you happy."

She stared at him intently, suddenly afraid to breathe. She had never heard those words from him before.

"Now I want you to hear what I have to say and then we'll talk."

She nodded, wondering what he had planned, remembering that Nick was a politician, so accustomed to saying what he thought people wanted to hear, able to talk people into seeing things his way. Yet there was a tiny part of her that was hanging on his every word because he had never offered to give up one thing for her happiness before.

"You want to stay in Houston, I know. I made a list of what you need and want—take care of your grandparents and continue running the three offices of the real estate business. Right?"

"Yes," she whispered, wondering what he would suggest.

"I'll tell you what I want. I've thought about my political career, my legal career in Dallas and the ranch. I love being a rancher and you made me stop and think. Why am I pursuing the others when ranching is what I love? But I can move to Houston and practice law there, and if I have to live in Houston to make you happy, I will."

She stared at him, barely able to breathe and wondering if she had heard him correctly. "You'd give up your political career?" she whispered.

"Absolutely. I'll do what I need to if it means you and Cody would be in my life. But now here is what I'm thinking—see if you would want this at all. I can move your grandparents with us to the ranch and get full-time care for your grandfather with as many nurses as you want. I can afford it. If it's not satisfactory to live on the ranch, we could live in Dallas where I can practice law. Your grandparents can live in our house."

She blinked as another shock hit her...*our house*...was that a convoluted proposal? "You're forget—"

"Shh. Wait until I'm through," he said, touching her lips lightly with his finger. "You can hire someone to run your business in Houston and you can open another one in Dallas. Between all the members of my family, we'll have more contacts than your grandfather did, so you'll not lack for customers. We know builders, too."

He stepped closer. "How am I doing so far?"

Dazed, she stared at him. "Pretty good. You covered my grandparents, my business, the ranch, your career—you left out one thing, Nick. Us. Me and Cody."

"I just wanted you to know what I'm willing to do before I get to us," he said. "Claire, I can't tell you how empty my life has been without you and Cody. I don't want to live that way." His hands slipped to her waist and he drew her closer.

"I love you, Claire. I love you with all my heart. I'll do whatever I need to do to make you happy."

Her heart thudded and her breath left her. "Nick," she gasped, wrapping her arms around his neck, fighting back tears. "You're really willing to do all of that?"

"If it gets me you and Cody, your love, yes, I am. You don't need to ask twice. I'll do what you want. I'm not losing you again. Will you marry me?"

"Nick," she said, her heart pounding with joy as she stood on tiptoe to kiss him.

His arms banded her and he held her tightly, leaning over her to kiss her. She couldn't stop tears of joy, of relief, thinking how much she had hurt just thinking of the empty nights ahead. Instead, Nick was willing to do whatever would make her happy so they could be together.

"Hey, darlin', you're crying. Don't cry. That's the last thing I intended. I don't want to hurt you ever again, Claire.

I promise. You tell me what you want. I love you. Will you marry me?" he repeated.

"Yes," she answered, smiling and still crying. "Nick, I've hurt so badly and wanted you so much. Yes, I'll marry you." She kissed him then.

When his words had had a moment to sink in, she asked him, "You really mean you're giving up politics after you finish this term of office?"

"I'm already finished. I resigned. It'll be in the news tomorrow, I'm sure."

Staring at him, she was stunned. "You resigned as a Texas State Representative?"

"Yes, I did. I thought we could work things out better if I gave that up right now."

"I'm stunned. You did that for me?"

"I want you to know that I mean all this. I love you, Claire, and I'm not losing you again."

"Have you told your dad?"

"Yes, I have, and he was delighted because he thinks now he'll get to see more of Cody, and Mom is even happier about it. Mom said she regrets that they didn't meet you when I was dating you."

"This is a day of one shock right after another," she said, looking at Nick. She kissed him, trying to convey the love she felt for him, love that she no longer tried to crush or ignore or deny. Stepping back, she gazed into the blue eyes that she loved. He'd taken a huge step, given up something important to him, just for her. Now it was her turn.

"Nick, I might want to commute and open a Dallas office after we get my grandparents settled, but if you want to be a rancher, I'll move to Verity. The ranch would be a wonderful place for Cody to grow up."

Nick leaned close to kiss her, drawing her tightly against him. She closed her eyes, kissing him with joy and love.

Happiness filled her as he leaned over her and kissed her passionately, and she held him tightly, thrilled that she had his love and they would be together, a family for Cody.

In minutes, she leaned back to look up at him. "You would really have moved to Houston for me?"

"Yes, ma'am, I would have. Whatever it takes to make you happy. I thought a lot about it and decided that all that was really important was the woman I love, my child, my family. That's true happiness for me."

"I'm amazed. I love you, Nick," she said before he kissed her.

When he released her, she gazed up at him. "Cody will be hyper when he finds out he's going to live on a ranch." She giggled then, feeling like an excited child herself. Then she realized she'd been remiss. "Nick, I need to ask my grandmother if they'll be willing to move. I want to ask my grandfather, too."

"Fine. You talk to them first, but then I will. I can afford to get whatever medical help we need for your grandfather. Think I should ask your grandfather for your hand in marriage?"

She laughed. "I don't think you need to, since we have a three-year-old son."

"Remember, you have an early Christmas present on the tree. You can open it now."

She looked at the small box tucked between the branches of rosemary. She pulled it out, carefully untying the ribbon while Nick showered light kisses on her temple, her ear, her throat. As she unwrapped the paper, he turned to watch when she raised the lid. A small black box was inside. She glanced at him and then pulled it out to open it. She gasped as she looked at the sparkling ring with one huge diamond surrounded by a circle of smaller stones.

"Oh, Nick. It's beautiful."

Nick took it from her, taking her hand. "I love you, Claire, with all my heart."

"I love you," she repeated, more tears of happiness falling.

She hugged him and he kissed her, picking her up tightly in his arms to carry her to bed.

Later, as she lay cradled against him, she ran her finger along his jaw, feeling the tiny stubble. "Nick, I love you so. There's never been another man since we first met. Not ever." She kissed away his answer, holding him tightly, feeling giddy with happiness.

"I'm going to spend a lifetime trying to make up to you for the breakup and the harsh words. I—"

She placed her fingers on his lips. "Shh. That's over and in the past, and we've moved on. Let it go, Nick, and I will, too. We're together now and that's what is important."

She rose slightly to look down at him. "Christmas is next week. What are your plans?"

"This year the whole family is going to Mom and Dad's for dinner on Christmas Eve. Christmas Day everyone is on their own. I'll be with you and your family that afternoon. Then everyone's invited to Wyatt's for dinner Christmas night."

"If you'd like, come Christmas Eve and join us. You'll miss dinner at your parents' house, but we'll be happy to have you."

"I accept," he said, kissing her briefly.

She rolled off the bed to gather her clothes. "Nick, I need to go home. I'm not spending the night here."

"Home, it is," he said.

She loved the sound of that word on his lips.

As Nick drove her home, she placed her hand on his knee. "Nick, we've never talked about children. We've lost some time. Cody is already three. I'd like Cody to have a sibling or two."

Nick smiled. "I think that's a marvelous idea. I agree. As soon as you want."

"I might want to just retire to the ranch with you and raise a family."

"That would suit me fine," he said.

She laughed. "Cody is going to be impossible to calm down. If he thinks he is moving to the ranch, he won't sleep for a week."

"So maybe we ought to both take the rest of the time until Christmas and go to the ranch. I can fly your grandmother and grandfather there, also his nurse and a caregiver, whoever you need to hire for him."

"I'll ask if they want to do that," she said, watching him drive and bubbling with happiness over the changes in her life. "I love you so much, Nick. You'll never ever know, even though I'm going to try to show you. Even though I've held out for things, I love you with all my heart."

"Tomorrow I'll come by and let's tell Cody the news." He snagged a quick kiss. "Get your camera ready."

Twelve

In a white silk dress with a square neckline, short sleeves and a narrow skirt that ended at her knees, Claire stood in the vestibule of her church in Houston. Her great-uncle stood beside her with her arm linked in his as they watched Cody walk down the aisle with the wedding ring.

In the front, on the aisle, sat her grandma. Next to her was Grandpa and beside him a nurse. A wheelchair was set out of the way temporarily.

When it was her turn to walk down the aisle, her gaze honed in on Nick, who had never looked more handsome in his black suit.

As Nick took her hand, he stepped close beside her to repeat their vows. Near them, Cody stood with a big smile. She glanced up at Nick who squeezed her hand.

As soon as they were pronounced man and wife, Nick picked up Cody and the three of them walked up the aisle to the vestibule where Nick turned so they could hug.

"I love you both with all my heart," Nick said gruffly.

Cody smiled. "I love you, too, you and Mama," he said, smiling at her.

"This is going to be good, Claire," Nick said. "I'll do my best to see that it is."

"I think it's going to be difficult to see who's the happiest—Cody or me," she answered.

"Let's get this reception over."

While the wedding had been small, the reception was large, filled with relatives and friends from all over Texas. The January party was held at a Houston country club. As the band played, Claire and Nick mingled with guests. At one point they stood in a Milan family gathering.

"You've been the miracle worker," Tony said, "getting my brother to finally take up ranching. If anyone had challenged me, I would have bet my spread that wouldn't ever happen."

Nick merely grinned and kept his arm around Claire's waist.

"I'm betting you never have a second's regret," Madison said, smiling at them.

"Well, my term as sheriff will be up before you know it, so if you need a political office, I can throw your hat—"

"Brother, stop right there," Nick said, grinning. "You can forget that one. Wait until Cody is old enough. I can't get him to stop wearing that little badge."

Wyatt smiled. "He can visit anytime he wants."

"We still need to get that kid to a rodeo," Tony stated.

"That's on my agenda," Nick said. "Once he sees one, he'll want to go all the time."

They stood laughing and talking, and at one point Madison took Claire's arm to walk away and leave the brothers. "I thought you might need a break from horse talk. Seriously, Claire, I've never seen Nick look as happy. Frankly, he didn't at his wedding to Karen. You and Cody are so good for him. He's way more laid-back now."

"I'm glad. I hope he doesn't have regrets. He gave up a lot."

"I don't think there's the slightest chance of that happening. These boys had a grandfather who caused them to all love being cowboys. It doesn't matter what kind of fortune the Milans have, those guys are happiest on the back of a horse or riding across the ranch in a pickup. You'll see. Nick will never look back. That was something our Dad wanted him to do—law and politics. Now, because of you, Nick's married his first love."

"Thanks, Madison. You make me feel good," Claire said, smiling.

"And here he comes, looking like a man ready to escape a party," Madison said, laughing and walking away.

Nick joined her. "I suppose I just ran Madison off."

"She didn't mind."

"I'm ready to bow out of this. They've already taken your grandfather home. Your grandmother and Irene are waiting with Cody for us to tell them goodbye and there's a limo to take them home. Can I get you to leave now?"

"Of course," she said, taking his hand. They walked out of the room and outside the club, where Grandma and Cody stood in the sunshine beside a white limousine. The tall gray-haired nanny stood nearby and smiled at Claire.

Claire stopped to speak briefly with Irene and then moved to Cody and her grandmother.

Claire picked up her son. "We'll be back at the end of the week. I promise to call you every night, and you tell Grandma if you want to call me. All right?"

"Yes, ma'am."

"I love you," she said, hugging him and loving the feel of his thin arms around her neck. She handed him over to Nick, who also gave him a big hug.

"We'll be back in a week," he said, setting Cody on his feet. Verna reached out to take his hand.

Claire hugged and kissed her grandmother and then climbed into the limo. Nick followed and the chauffeur closed the door behind him. They waved as they drove away, and then Nick pulled her into his arms.

"Mrs. Nick Milan. I've waited a long time for this, Claire. I love you," he said as he pulled her close again to kiss her.

"I love you, Nick," she whispered. Claire clung to him tightly while she kissed him. Joy filled her and she hoped they could give Cody a little brother and a little sister. She squeezed Nick tightly, still astounded that she was married to the man she had always loved. Like the diamonds on her finger, happiness held a glittering promise of her future with Nick and Cody. Her family.

* * * * *

If you loved this LONE STAR LEGENDS *novel,*
read more in this series from
USA TODAY *bestselling author Sara Orwig.*

THE TEXAN'S FORBIDDEN FIANCÉE
A TEXAN IN HER BED
AT THE RANCHER'S REQUEST
KISSED BY A RANCHER

Available now from Harlequin Desire!

If you're on Twitter, tell us what you think of
Harlequin Desire! #harlequindesire

COMING NEXT MONTH FROM

HARLEQUIN® *Desire*

Available January 5, 2016

#2419 TWIN HEIRS TO HIS THRONE
Billionaires and Babies • by Olivia Gates
Prince Voronov disappeared after he broke Kassandra's heart, leaving her pregnant and alone. Now the future king has returned to claim his twin heirs. Will he reclaim Kassandra's heart as part of the bargain?

#2420 NANNY MAKES THREE
Texas Cattleman's Club: Lies and Lullabies
by Cat Schield
Hadley Stratton is more than the nanny Liam Ward hired for his unexpected newborn niece. She's also the girl who got away...and the rich rancher is not going to let that happen twice!

#2421 A BABY FOR THE BOSS
Pregnant by the Boss • by Maureen Child
Is his one-time fling and current employee guilty of corporate espionage? Billionaire boss Mike Ryan believes so, but he'll need to reevaluate everything when he learns she's carrying his child...

#2422 PREGNANT BY THE RIVAL CEO
by Karen Booth
Anna Langford wants the deal—even though it means working with the guy she's never forgotten. But what starts as business turns into romance—until Anna learns of Jacob's ruthless motives and her unplanned pregnancy!

#2423 THAT NIGHT WITH THE RICH RANCHER
Lone Star Legends • by Sara Orwig
Tony can't believe the vision in red who won him at the bachelor auction. One night with Lindsay—his stubborn next-door neighbor—is all he'd signed up for. But her makeover has him forgetting all about their family feud!

#2424 TRAPPED WITH THE TYCOON
Mafia Moguls • by Jules Bennett
All that stands between mafia boss Braden O'Shea and what he wants is employee Zara Perkins. But when they're snowed in together, seduction becomes his only goal. Will he choose his family...or the woman he can't resist?

YOU CAN FIND MORE INFORMATION ON UPCOMING HARLEQUIN® TITLES, FREE EXCERPTS AND MORE AT WWW.HARLEQUIN.COM.

HDCNM1215

REQUEST YOUR FREE BOOKS!
2 FREE NOVELS PLUS 2 FREE GIFTS!

⊕ HARLEQUIN®

Desire

ALWAYS POWERFUL, PASSIONATE AND PROVOCATIVE

YES! Please send me 2 FREE Harlequin® Desire novels and my 2 FREE gifts (gifts are worth about $10). After receiving them, if I don't wish to receive any more books, I can return the shipping statement marked "cancel." If I don't cancel, I will receive 6 brand-new novels every month and be billed just $4.55 per book in the U.S. or $5.24 per book in Canada. That's a savings of at least 13% off the cover price! It's quite a bargain! Shipping and handling is just 50¢ per book in the U.S. and 75¢ per book in Canada.* I understand that accepting the 2 free books and gifts places me under no obligation to buy anything. I can always return a shipment and cancel at any time. Even if I never buy another book, the two free books and gifts are mine to keep forever.

225/326 HDN GH2P

Name	(PLEASE PRINT)	

Address		Apt. #

City	State/Prov.	Zip/Postal Code

Signature (if under 18, a parent or guardian must sign)

Mail to the **Reader Service:**
IN U.S.A.: P.O. Box 1867, Buffalo, NY 14240-1867
IN CANADA: P.O. Box 609, Fort Erie, Ontario L2A 5X3

Want to try two free books from another line?
Call 1-800-873-8635 or visit www.ReaderService.com.

* Terms and prices subject to change without notice. Prices do not include applicable taxes. Sales tax applicable in N.Y. Canadian residents will be charged applicable taxes. Offer not valid in Quebec. This offer is limited to one order per household. Not valid for current subscribers to Harlequin Desire books. All orders subject to credit approval. Credit or debit balances in a customer's account(s) may be offset by any other outstanding balance owed by or to the customer. Please allow 4 to 6 weeks for delivery. Offer available while quantities last.

Your Privacy—The Reader Service is committed to protecting your privacy. Our Privacy Policy is available online at www.ReaderService.com or upon request from the Reader Service.

We make a portion of our mailing list available to reputable third parties that offer products we believe may interest you. If you prefer that we not exchange your name with third parties, or if you wish to clarify or modify your communication preferences, please visit us at www.ReaderService.com/consumerschoice or write to us at Reader Service Preference Service, P.O. Box 9062, Buffalo, NY 14240-9062. Include your complete name and address.

HD15

SPECIAL EXCERPT FROM

HARLEQUIN
Desire

Prince Voronov disappeared after he broke Kassandra's heart, leaving her pregnant and alone. Now the future king has returned to claim his twin heirs. Will he reclaim Kassandra's heart, as well?

Read on for a sneak peek of
TWIN HEIRS TO HIS THRONE,
the latest in Olivia Gates*'s*
BILLIONAIRES OF BLACK CASTLES series.

Kassandra fumbled for the remote, pushing every button before she managed to turn off the TV.

But it was too late. She'd seen him. For the first time since she'd walked out of his hospital room twenty-six months ago. That had been the last time the world had seen him, too. He'd dropped off the radar completely ever since. Now her retinas burned with the image of Leonid striding out of his imposing Fifth Avenue headquarters.

The man she'd known had been crackling with vitality, a smile of whimsy and assurance always hovering on his lips and sparkling in the depths of his eyes. This man was totally detached, as if he was no longer part of the world. Or as if it was beneath his notice. And there'd been another change. The stalking swagger was gone. In its place was a deliberate, almost menacing prowl.

This wasn't the man she'd known.

Or rather, the man she'd thought she'd known.

She'd long ago faced the fact that she'd known nothing of him. Not before she'd been with him, or while they'd been together, or after he'd shoved her away and vanished.

Kassandra had withdrawn from the world, too. She'd been pathetic enough to be literally sick with worry about him, to pine for him until she'd wasted away. Until she'd almost miscarried. That scare had finally jolted her to the one reality she'd been certain of. That she'd wanted that baby with everything in her and would never risk losing it. That day at the doctor's, she'd found out she wasn't carrying one baby, but two.

She'd reclaimed herself and her stability, had become even more successful career-wise, but most important, she'd become a mother to two perfect daughters. Eva and Zoya. She'd given them both names meaning life, as they'd given *her* new life.

Then Zorya had suddenly filled the news with a declaration of its intention to reinstate the monarchy. With every rapid development, foreboding had filled her. Even when she'd had no reason to think it would make Leonid resurface.

The doorbell rang.

It had become a ritual for her neighbor to come by and have a cup of tea so they could unwind together after their hectic days.

Rushing to the door, she opened it with a ready smile. "We should…"

Air clogged her lungs. All her nerves fired, short-circuiting her every muscle, especially her heart.

Leonid.

Right there. On her doorstep.

Don't miss TWIN HEIRS TO HS THRONE
by USA TODAY bestselling author Olivia Gates,
available January 2016 wherever
Harlequin® Desire books and ebooks are sold.

www.Harlequin.com

Copyright © 2016 by Olivia Gates

HDEXP1215

Turn your love of reading into rewards you'll love with
Harlequin My Rewards

**Join for FREE today at
www.HarlequinMyRewards.com**

Earn **FREE BOOKS** of your choice.

Experience **EXCLUSIVE OFFERS** and contests.

Enjoy **BOOK RECOMMENDATIONS**
selected just for you.

PLUS! Sign up now
and get **500** points
right away!

Earn **FREE** REWARDS
Join Today!
HarlequinMyRewards.com

MYR16R

Love the Harlequin book you just read?

Your opinion matters.

Review this book on your favorite book site, review site, blog or your own social media properties and share your opinion with other readers!

Be sure to connect with us at:
Harlequin.com/Newsletters
Facebook.com/HarlequinBooks
Twitter.com/HarlequinBooks

HREVIEWS

THE WORLD IS BETTER WITH

Romance

Harlequin has everything from contemporary, passionate and heartwarming to suspenseful and inspirational stories.

Whatever your mood, we have a romance just for you!

Connect with us to find your next great read, special offers and more.

 /HarlequinBooks

 @HarlequinBooks

www.HarlequinBlog.com

www.Harlequin.com/Newsletters

HARLEQUIN®

A *Romance* FOR EVERY MOOD™

www.Harlequin.com

SERIESHALOAD2015

HARLEQUIN®

A *Romance* FOR EVERY MOOD™

JUST CAN'T GET ENOUGH?

Join our social communities
and talk to us online.

You will have access to the latest
news on upcoming titles and special
promotions, but most importantly,
you can talk to other fans about your
favorite Harlequin reads.

Harlequin.com/Community

f Facebook.com/HarlequinBooks

𝕏 Twitter.com/HarlequinBooks

𝓟 Pinterest.com/HarlequinBooks

HSOCIAL